He laughed and the sound so surprised her she almost missed the smile that made little crinkly lines at the corner of his eyes and creased his left cheek where a dimple suddenly appeared. Now why hadn't she noticed the dimple earlier?

She was a sucker for dimples.

"It's a new trend. By the end of the week anyone who's anyone will have a big dent in the front of their car, too."

So, the man had a sense of humor. Surprise, surprise. Of course it only added to her... Her what? Infatuation? No, absolutely not. Morbid curiosity. Yes, morbid curiosity. "What's a guy like you doing in a place like this?"

"Isn't that my line?"

"Oh, that's easy, I live here. But you probably already know that because I gave you my address this morning. Remember?"

"As if I could forget. Your car was glued to mine at the time."

"As I recall it was because I was on my cell phone. Did I tell you I don't own a cell phone?"

She got a lot of satisfaction out of his wince.

"Where's your car?"

"It broke. Can't fix it."

"And you're walking home from work?"

She wanted to close her eyes in mortification. So he had seen her at the bookstore. Why could she never find a good sinkhole when she needed one? "Looks like it."

He reached over the passenger seat and popped open the car door. "Get in."

Accidental Love

by

Sharon Cullen

This is a work of fiction. Names, characters, places, and incidents either are the product of the author's imagination or are used fictitiously, and any resemblance to actual persons living or dead, business establishments, events, or locales, is entirely coincidental.

Accidental Love

COPYRIGHT © 2008 by Sharon Cullen

All rights reserved. No part of this book may be used or reproduced in any manner whatsoever without written permission of the author or The Wild Rose Press except in the case of brief quotations embodied in critical articles or reviews.
Contact Information: info@thewildrosepress.com

Cover Art by *Angela Anderson*

The Wild Rose Press
PO Box 708
Adams Basin, NY 14410-0706
Visit us at www.thewildrosepress.com

Publishing History
First Champagne Rose Edition, 2008
Print ISBN 1-60154-293-3

Published in the United States of America

Praise for Sharon Cullen

Sharon Cullen takes a penetrating look into the lasting effect of labels placed on vulnerable young people. Strong characterization and a red-hot romance combine to turn *Hands Off* into a steamy and intriguing read.
~ 4 Hearts, Night Owl Romance Book Reviews

"...a heartwarming story, showing the true power of love."
~ The Romance Studio on *The Power of Love*

"The beauty in the story comes from the message of hope and love delivered by Sharon Cullen. I finished this book in a very short amount of time, but it has left me with a smile in my heart which truly is *The Power of Love*."
~ Two Lips Reviews

"*The Power of Love*" is an unusual and, well, powerful love story.
~ Sweetness and Light Reviews

"I found *The Power of Love* to be a very interesting story with an intriguing plotline...I will definitely keep Sharon Cullen on my list of authors to watch."
~ Joyfully Reviewed

"...a heartwarming story, showing the true power of love."
~ The Romance Studio on *The Power of Love*

The Power of Love was nominated for a 2007 CAPA

Dedication

To John,
who drove a rusted out Datsun when we first met.
For all the memories we created in that car.
Twenty-four years later and
I love you more every day.

Chapter 1

Nathan stomped on the brake. The Porsche's tires squealed. Metal scraped against metal and he was thrown forward, forcing his seatbelt to lock and throwing him back as the cars collided.

In the quiet aftermath, Nathan stared, stunned, at the side of the battered car crumpled against his Porsche.

He yanked on the door handle, climbed out, and scowled at the rusted Datsun 210. It had taken the brunt of the impact. Served the driver right for turning in front of him.

Traffic, momentarily stopped, began to veer around the two cars, the drivers honking their displeasure, some even yelling at them. Nathan had an uncontrollable urge to flip them the bird.

Crouching beside his car, he rested his elbows on his knees and stared. The rust bucket's front fender nestled nicely in the groove it had carved out for itself in the quarter panel of his damn Porsche.

Son of a bitch.

He straightened and eyed the two cars, fused together like lovers. It was hard to tell for sure, but the 210 looked like it had once been white. The paint had long ago given way to rust, however. Of course, someone who owned a car like this probably didn't have insurance. Wonderful. Fucking wonderful.

He strode over to the driver's door of the 210 and jerked it open. The door screeched. A sound not too far off from nails on a chalkboard.

He took a step back as one long leg poked

out. Absently, he noticed the owner of the leg wore bright red toe nail polish that matched her bright red flip-flop, but he was more intrigued by the leg. Her calf and thigh were well toned, and nicely tanned. Another leg came out, matching its predecessor and, before he knew it, the whole she-bang was out of the car and standing before him.

Slowly, his gaze traveled up those gorgeous legs and paused at the cut-off denims. A red tank top stopped a few inches above the shorts and a belly button ring winked at him as the sun's rays hit it. Nathan found himself biting back a grin at the red and gold ladybug perched in the hollow of the sexiest navel he'd ever seen.

His gaze continued on to a spectacular pair of breasts. Firm and well rounded, with nipples poking through the thin material of the tank top.

Curly blond hair was pulled back in a ponytail and topped with a Cincinnati Reds baseball hat. Several pair of earrings glittered in each ear. Finally, his eyes met hers and he wasn't disappointed with those either. Light brown. No, not brown, but gold with flecks of green. Damn, they were the most gorgeous eyes he'd ever seen.

A passing car honked, yanking Nathan out of a sexual pull so strong he'd forgotten where he was.

A busy intersection.

His dented Porsche.

"I'm really sorry..." The woman waved her hand toward the two cars. There was a light tinkling as a half dozen or so bracelets slid down her arm.

"Where the hell was your head?" he growled, eager to latch on to his anger and frustration rather than wallow in what was way too close to lust. "You turned right in front of me."

She paled under her golden tan. "I'm sorry—"

"Never mind." He swept her explanations away with a short chopping motion of his hand and turned to survey the cars. He didn't want to hear her excuses. More than likely, she'd been either talking on her cell phone or texting. "There's not enough damage to call the police. We'll just exchange information and contact our insurance companies." He narrowed his eyes at her. "You do have insurance, right?"

"Sure, it's just—"

"Good." He glanced at his watch and grimaced. "Because I'm late for an appointment. Could we hurry this along?"

She turned and dove through the driver's side of the 210 to open her glove box. Nathan pulled his gaze from the sight of the cut-offs hugging a heart-shaped ass that made his mouth water and marched to his own car, found the necessary documents neatly tucked into the glove box with a pad of paper and pen, and marched back.

Blondie was standing beside her car, muttering to herself as she searched through a stack of papers fused together with what looked like coffee that had spilled long ago. She pulled out an insurance card and dropped her license. Sighing, he bent to retrieve it only to have the whole mess of papers fall on his head and shoulders and scatter between his feet.

"Oh, sorry," she said, bending to help him retrieve them.

He handed the sticky papers to her and straightened.

She stood as well, clutching her driver's license and the papers, watching him with wary brown eyes.

He shoved the pen and paper at her. "Write down your info and I'll do the same. Then we can get the hell out of here."

She tried to juggle her papers and take his pen and pad. "Here, give me those," he said, taking the papers from her.

He noted her bold handwriting and was relieved to see she didn't dot her i's with flowers or hearts. She handed him the pen and paper and he handed her the license and other junk. What a frickin' circus. After writing his own information and handing it to her, he noted she put it on top of the other papers. Great, now she'd lose it.

"Thank you Miss—" He glanced at the info in his hand. "Hollis. You'll be hearing from my insurance company. Can't say it's been a pleasure, but..." He couldn't help himself, he looked over her magnificent body one more time. "It sure has been interesting." His gaze stopped at golden eyes narrowed in what appeared to be anger. He didn't know what she had to be angry about. She was the one who'd turned in front of him and he was being damn gracious by not calling the cops and having her cited. "Next time stay off the cell phone and maybe this won't happen," he said.

Amber sparks flew from her eyes before she looked at the paper in her hand. "Thank you, *Mister* Gardner." It was clear she thought he didn't deserve the title.

"You're right," she said. "It sure has been interesting. And enlightening." She turned to climb back into her 210. It took a few tries to get the engine to turn over and, for a moment, Nathan thought he'd have to give her a lift somewhere. The idea both intrigued him and irritated him.

****

Dani glanced in her rearview mirror to see Mr. Personality slide into his car and drive in the opposite direction.

At the next stoplight, she rested her wrists on top of the steering wheel and stared out the front windshield. *Damn, damn, damn.*

She hadn't heard the last of Nathan Gardner. Too soon, he'd realize the insurance information she'd given him was false. Well, not exactly false. Just not...current. As in expired. Way expired.

Dani shivered in apprehension as the light turned green and she accelerated through, her engine making a funny pinging sound.

It's his own damn fault. She had every intention of telling him, and assuring him she'd pay for the damages herself, but he'd gone all high and mighty, not letting her speak, acting as if she were some dumb blond without the sense God gave her.

"Stay off the cell phone my ass," she muttered as she sped through a yellow light and snorted.

What a condescending prick. What an arrogant, self-centered, over-bearing, vain and...and... Her usually impressive vocabulary failed her after vain and she settled on prick again.

And just how much would it cost to repair a Porsche 911 Turbo? Damn near all her savings. Probably more. *Darn it, Dani, of all the cars you had to run in to, it would have to be an expensive sports car wouldn't it?*

Chapter 2

"Well?" Dani asked. "What's wrong? Can you fix it?" Her brother, Ted, shook his head, reached for the beer on the fender of her now dead car, and took a long swallow. "Nope," he said, wiping his mouth with the back of his hand and leaving a grease mark on his upper lip.

"What do you mean you can't fix it?" She needed a car to get to and from work. She needed to get to and from work in order to pay the bills and eat. Oh, yeah. And pay for the damages done to the Porsche.

"I think you cracked your engine block."

"How did I crack the engine block? I wasn't going *that* fast."

Ted shrugged and took another swig of beer. "Don't know. I'm not an expert on these things." He shook his head. "A Porsche 911 Turbo."

He'd been saying that ever since she called and asked him to look at her car.

"Good thing you have insurance. You know what a 911 Turbo cost these days?"

No, but she could guess. William had bought a used Carrera when they'd been dating and it hadn't been cheap. She doubted Nathan Gardner bought anything used.

"What am I supposed to do now?" It took every bit of her Herculean control to keep the panic out of her voice. She clenched her fingers into a fist, her nails biting into the palm of her hand. For a moment, one tiny moment, she allowed herself to regret the decision to leave

New York and return to her hometown before pushing the thought away.

"Buy a new car," Ted said. "We've been telling you for a year now, you need a more reliable car." Ted began gathering his tools.

"I can't afford a new car and you know it."

Ted paused and glanced at her, worry in his hazel eyes. "Let us help you, Dani. Mom and Dad—"

"No."

"Damn it—"

"I said no." She turned to her sister who'd been watching the exchange quietly. "Can I borrow your car tonight, Sammy?"

"Sorry, Dan, it's my night to volunteer at the hospital."

Dani turned to Ted who was already shaking his head. "Hot date."

Oh, sure, Ted was all about Mom and Dad helping her, but when it came to him driving her somewhere he wouldn't give up his "hot date." She shouldn't bitch. Her entire family had rallied around her when she'd returned home so unexpectedly. They'd been nothing but supportive, if not a little suffocating. She bit her bottom lip and picked through her options, finally settling on the only one available. "Sammy, can you at least take me to work and bring me home?"

"Sure, I guess. I'll have to leave the hospital early, but they shouldn't mind."

She eyed her sister in trepidation. "Will you remember to come get me?" Sammy had a habit of forgetting important things.

Her sister rolled her eyes. "Yes, I'll remember. Get your things."

****

Butt stuck in the air, cheek pressed to the

floor, arm under the shelving unit, Dani reached as far as possible. Her fingers just barely brushed the book that had fallen behind the shelf when she heard his voice.

Closing her eyes tightly, she prayed he wasn't standing behind her. Why the hell was he in *her* bookstore? And the children's section of all places?

Carefully, slowly, she extracted her arm and rose to her knees to peek around the corner of the shelf.

A tall woman with black hair, dressed in a black pencil thin skirt and black satin jacket, all by Donna Karan, stepped into Dani's line of sight. The woman's fingernails glittered as she waved them about while she spoke to her companion.

Dani's gaze traveled to the companion and her heart did a funny little lurch.

Nathan Gardner's hair was that sexy combination of brown with streaks of blond and red highlights. It was shaggy, the strands tossed about and Dani decided the look fit him.

He was still dressed in the Gianni Manzoni suit he'd worn during their...altercation...earlier in the day. Men who wore Italian-made suits and hand-made leather shoes, exuding power and lethal charm, were either limp fish who needed pretty dressings to make them feel important or power hungry machines who chewed up and spit out anyone who dared to get close.

Gardner was definitely not a limp fish. That meant he was the power hungry machine.

Gardner glanced in her direction and Dani shuffled out of sight. She pressed her eyes shut. Oh, God. How embarrassing to be caught on her knees staring and eavesdropping. Hopefully he hadn't seen her.

She stood and edged around the back of the children's section, keeping to the shelves and in the shadows, until she was in the opposite aisle from them.

The two turned and wandered to the other side of the store, leaving Dani alone to stare after them.

****

Nathan pulled his dented Porsche into the driveway of Veronica's condo and cut the ignition. The rumble of the engine immediately stopped, plunging them into silence.

Beside him, Veronica reached for her purse and bag of books she'd bought for her niece's birthday. "You coming in?" she asked.

He stared out the front window. A clinch in his gut told him he'd reached a turning point in his life. He could go inside and secure his future, or... He could refuse and walk a path he'd never anticipated walking. He drew in a deep breath. "No."

A heavy silence followed, thick with disappointment. Disapproval.

"Okay," she said, her voice hard and cold and a little perplexed.

This wasn't their normal routine. After every date, Veronica invited him in for drinks. Drinks led to an invitation to stay the night.

Ordinarily, he'd accept both the drink and the sex.

The jeweler's box lay inside his pocket, heavy against his thigh. The appointment he'd been late for, because of a certain curly-haired blond named Dani Hollis, had been to pick up the one-of-a-kind engagement ring.

Veronica was his perfect companion. She had her own career as a defense attorney. She wasn't needy or clingy, but practical and self-sufficient.

And suddenly Nathan wanted none of that.

Visions of an impish smile and brown eyes peering around the corner of a rack of books popped into his head, but it wasn't Dani Hollis who had prompted this decision. A lot of things had, and to be honest, he'd been heading down this particular road for a long time. He'd thought buying the ring would somehow make things clearer, but it had only heightened his anxiety and made him realize no matter how perfect Veronica seemed, she wasn't what he wanted.

He twisted in his seat and took Veronica's hand in his, staring at the long fingernails painted a horrific shade of red that reminded him of blood. "I'm sorry, Veronica, but this...relationship...it's just not working for me."

Veronica pressed her lips together—blood red lips to match her blood red fingernails. "I can't say I'm not sorry, Nathan. We could be good together."

Good, yes. Great? Doubtful. He hadn't even told her he loved her.

Love? He could almost hear his father's snort of disapproval. *What does love have to do with it, Nathan? It's an alliance. A solid alliance.*

But Nathan didn't want an alliance. He wasn't some damn country in need of economic reform. He wanted love.

"I want better than good," he said.

Veronica stared at him for a few tense moments, her expression calm, thoughtful. "You'll be back," she said matter-of-factly. "Things moved too fast. Your father... I know how he can be, Nathan. I'm not blind. He pushed for this."

That was true, but Nathan didn't want to give her false hope. "Veronica—"

She opened the door. "Believe it or not, I

understand," she said, her serious gaze going to his. She was always serious, he realized. Had he ever seen her laugh? A great, big belly laugh with tears rolling down her face? Better yet, when was the last time *he'd* laughed like that?

"You know where to find me when you change your mind," she said as she got out of the car.

She made her way to her front door and Nathan watched her go, a little stunned, a lot perplexed, but more relieved. He couldn't figure out what surprised him more. That he'd broken it off with her or that she assumed he'd be back. So what *had* he expected? Her to fall all over him and demand an explanation? Not like her. She was too controlled. Self-contained.

Sanitized.

That's the word he'd been looking for. Definitely not the way to describe your wife. "Hello, this is my wife, Veronica. She's...sanitized."

He laughed in the quiet of the car and wondered if he was going nuts. The best thing that ever happened to him just walked into her condo without a backward glance.

When Nathan pulled out of Veronica's driveway, he slid a Rolling Stones CD into the changer, cranked the volume, and drove away. He cracked the windows, letting in the warm, fall air.

Cruising to the Stones, he contemplated his next action. One option was to hit the uptown bars, search out a few friends, and down a nice imported beer. Or go into the office and tackle the stack of paperwork waiting for him.

His mind switched gears as golden eyes flashed before him.

He'd seen Dani at the bookstore, peeking

around the corner. For a moment, those big amber eyes had frozen him. But then, she'd disappeared and he'd had this crazy urge to find her. He'd never met anyone like her, all fire and ice.

That was all it was. Fascination. Hell, who knows, maybe some part of him was rebelling. That would explain the whole Veronica break-up. And sure as shit, Dani Hollis was one-hundred and eighty degrees different than any woman he'd had.

Not that he wanted her. Hadn't he just extricated himself from one relationship? And quite nicely, thank you very much. He sure as hell didn't need another. Not with flighty Dani Hollis.

Yet, he felt bad for the way he'd treated her earlier. Even if she hadn't been paying attention, talking on a cell phone or whatever, that was no reason to be so rude. Hell, his own attention had wandered a few times while driving. He should apologize at the very least.

He knew where she lived. One glance at the address and telephone number she'd given him and he'd memorized it all. Shit, who was he kidding? Her information was seared onto his brain. He headed toward her street, wondering what the hell he was doing. A phone call would do well enough. Or flowers sent by his secretary with a nicely worded apology.

He kept driving.

She lived about as far from him as she could get both geographically and economically. Her street was on the edge of a not-so-safe neighborhood where violence frequently erupted, where men hung out on street corners in the middle of the day and women hung out at night. For some reason, the thought of her living so close to something that could easily hurt her bothered him.

He snorted at his white knight attitude. An attitude that would surely have flames sparking from her golden eyes. He didn't even know the woman, for Christ's sake. What little he did know was that she didn't pay attention when she drove and she worked in a bookstore.

And she sported a ladybug belly-button ring.

Slowly, he cruised the main street of her neighborhood, passing store windows taped with yellowed newspapers. Trash littered the cracked sidewalks and choked the sewers. Abandoned cars dotted the side of the road. A lone figure walked with determination along the darkened street and Nathan did one of those comic-book double takes.

He slowed the car to a crawl and pulled alongside Dani.

She began to walk faster in a desperate-to-escape half-walk, half-run. Her purse was slung over her shoulder, held tightly to her chest in a white knuckled grip.

He hit the button to lower the passenger side window and called her name.

Chapter 3

Dani had heard the car behind her and gripped the strap of her purse tighter. *Don't look people in the eye, just keep walking.*

In this part of town, that was a good motto to live by.

She cursed her sister for forgetting to pick her up, cursed Nathan Gardner for cracking her engine block, even though she'd been at fault, cursed her manager for leaving before he knew for certain she had a ride home, and for good measure cursed her brother for not being able to fix her car.

After all the cursing, she concentrated on walking fast and keeping an eye on the entrance to an alley looming before her.

"Dani? Is that you?"

Her step faltered and she cursed silently. Why was *he* in her end of town and how had he found her?

The nearly silent purr of his powerful engine kept pace. She stopped, walked over to the car, and leaned into the passenger side window, plastering on a wide smile. "Nice car. Did you know you have a big dent in the front?"

He laughed and the sound so surprised her that she almost missed the smile that made little crinkly lines at the corner of his eyes and creased his left cheek where a dimple suddenly appeared. Now why hadn't she noticed the dimple earlier? She was a sucker for dimples.

"It's a new trend. By the end of the week,

anyone who's anyone will have a big dent in the front of their car, too."

So, the man had a sense of humor. Surprise, surprise. Of course it only added to her... Her what? Infatuation? No, absolutely not. Morbid curiosity. Yes, morbid curiosity. "What's a guy like you doing in a place like this?"

"Isn't that my line?"

"Oh, that's easy, I live here. But you probably already know that because I gave you my address this morning. Remember?"

"As if I could forget. Your car was glued to mine at the time."

"Yeah, as I recall it was because I was on my cell phone. Did I tell you I don't own a cell phone?"

She got a lot of satisfaction out of his wince. "Listen, Dani, I'm sorry for my rude behavior this morning. It was uncalled for."

The unexpected apology threw her. To cover her surprise, she shrugged. "Forget it. I made you late for an important appointment. Did you make it by the way?"

"Make what?"

"The appointment."

His gaze flickered and she could have sworn something sad passed through his eyes, but it was gone before she had time to comprehend it.

"Yes. I made the appointment."

"Good. Well, see ya 'round." She straightened and thumped the top of his car.

"Where's your car?"

"I cracked the engine block or something. It broke. Can't fix it."

His eyes grew wide. "And you're walking home from work?"

She wanted to close her eyes in mortification. So he *had* seen her at the bookstore. Why could she never find a good sinkhole when she needed one? "Looks like it."

He reached over the passenger seat and popped open the car door. "Get in."

She hesitated.

"Get in, Dani."

She inspected the deserted streets, the darkened doorways of abandoned businesses, and the meager streetlights, most of which were busted. Then she took a long look at the car. Walk or ride. Walk or ride. Really, there was no choice. She could kill Sammy for forgetting about her.

"Only if you say please," she said, her gaze sliding back to his.

Beautifully sculpted lips lifted in a half-smile. "Dani. Please. Get in the car."

She hesitated some more, hating the thought of sitting beside this man in such a small car. What she hated worse was she didn't know why she hated the thought of sitting beside this man in such a small car.

Yes she did. She knew. It was the Porsche and the Italian business suit. It was the air of authority and the stink of "rich-man" oozing from his pores.

"This isn't the safest street to walk late at night," he said, and she wanted to wipe the sincerity out of his voice, the concern off his face. Men like him weren't concerned with women like her. Not unless they wanted something.

"I'm okay," she said. "I lived in the Big Apple for seven years. I can handle this measly street."

"Get in before I throw you in." His grin took the sting out of his words.

Voices emerged from the dark alley she'd been preparing to cross in front of. He was right. This wasn't the safest street late at night. With the voices getting closer, she hopped in and closed the door. It shut with a satisfying thunk and not a cat's screech like her clunker.

Nathan put the car in gear and smoothly pulled away from the curb. "I lived in New York, too."

"Really?" She infused her voice with a cool frost, informing him she didn't care to talk about New York. It was stupid of her to have even mentioned it.

The small sports car left no room between them and, every time he shifted gears, their arms brushed, sending goosebumps tingling up her spine.

By the time he pulled in front of her apartment, she had her hand on the door handle, ready to jump out. He touched her arm and she tensed.

Oh, please, please don't touch me. She was holding on by a thread. Memories still too raw threatened her and she wanted nothing more than to hide in her apartment, just like she'd hidden for the past year.

Nathan must have sensed her inward flinch because he pulled back. Dani looked at her arm then at him.

"Are you going to get a new car?" he asked.

She pasted on a smile. "What is this? First my brother and sister, now you. No, I'm not going to get a new car. It's not in the budget."

"So you're going to walk to work? Don't be absurd, Dani, it's a good eight blocks."

She was fast barreling down on getting pissed. The last thing she needed was Nathan Gardner sticking his nose in her life. "What business is it of yours whether I walk or fly on my broom stick?"

"When do you have to be at work again?"

"Why? Are you going to chauffeur me or send your chauffeur to drive me?"

When he didn't answer, she waved her hand in the air, tired of the conversation, and hating that she sounded like a shrew. "I'm sorry. I'm being bitchy."

"After the way I treated you this afternoon, I deserve it."

Dani puffed out a frustrated breath. She didn't want to like him, but he was making it damn hard. If he'd act like the jerk he'd been this morning, she could hide behind her devil-may-care attitude and hold tight to her belief that he was like all the other rich men she'd met. Like William.

But he was being nice and, on top of that, he could be funny. The combination ate at her prickly veneer and, now more than before, she wanted to run into her apartment and lock the door against him.

"Don't worry about me," she said. "My sister was supposed to pick me up tonight, but obviously something happened." Like she forgot. "Thanks for the lift."

She turned to open the door, but his hand on her arm stopped her again. She twisted to look over her shoulder and before she knew it, she was turned back around, his hands on her shoulders, his lips crushing hers.

Holey-moley. His hot tongue probed the seam of her lips and she opened for him, their tongues tangling, all fire and brimstone and volcanic eruptions that touched each synapse of her nervous system. Somehow, her hands made it to his shirt where she fisted the fine fabric. Hells bells, his chest was like silk spread over iron—hard and chiseled and warm. It made her wonder if other parts were just as hard, just as hot.

Accidental Love

Instantly, her own body heated until she was sure she would internally combust, sending sparks shooting from her ears. She was wet, willing, and ready—completely aware they shouldn't be doing this, but totally unable to stop it. Damn her traitorous body.

His gaze bore into hers when he pulled away, if possible looking more surprised than she felt. His lips glistened in the weak light of the street lamp he'd parked under. His hands were still on her shoulders and they stared at each other for long seconds, their breaths coming fast and furious.

Dani licked her lips, her stomach churning. Kissing Nathan Gardner was such a bad idea on so many levels, she couldn't even begin to name them. Didn't want to name them because then she'd have to admit that William Delaney had screwed with her in more ways than one. "Uh..."

"Shit." He let go of her and swiped a hand through his hair, dropping his head back against the headrest and looking at the ceiling. "Shit.'"

Hand shaking, she reached for the door handle again. Maybe she could sneak out and he wouldn't notice.

"Dani..." His voice was tense, thick. She shook her head and climbed out. She didn't want to hear what he had to say. It would be something along the lines of what a mistake their kiss had been and, while she knew that, she didn't want to hear him confirm it.

She stepped out of the car and shut the door, feeling his sizzling gaze on her back as she let herself into her apartment building.

Chapter 4

Monday morning dawned dreary and rainy. A perfect forecast for Nathan's less than perfect mood. And a more than perfect day to hold a particularly boring advertising meeting. He suppressed a yawn and doodled on his legal pad as the executives around him debated the merit of pouring more money into the advertising budget.

He should listen. Pay attention. But he couldn't keep his mind on track.

He hadn't had a very productive weekend either. Not after that kiss. What a mistake. Jumping headlong into one relationship ten minutes after extricating himself from another was not a smart move. But, man, that kiss... It'd been like the Fourth of July, Christmas, and his birthday all rolled into one. Skyrockets, softly falling snow, and endless surprises.

He'd lain awake for two nights reliving it. Stumbled through an entire Sunday remembering it.

"Mr. Gardner?"

Startled out if his musings, he looked around the conference table at the various pairs of eyes staring back. Some in confusion, most in disapproval, reminding him that he needed to get his shit together if he wanted to succeed in his newly minted position of CEO of Gardner Securities and Investments.

Most of the men around this table had sat here with his father, had watched Nathan grow

Accidental Love

up, and didn't believe he could run the business as well as the old man. It was his job to convince them.

He cleared his throat, sat straighter in his chair, and tapped his pen against the doodles on his legal pad. His face heated and, in the back of his mind, he heard his father's voice. *Nathan, pay attention. Good God, son, get your head out of the clouds for once.*

"I'm sorry, gentlemen. I was thinking about this new advertising campaign."

"Yes, well, we were discussing that ourselves." This came from Craig Howard, Vice President of Marketing. He launched into a long soliloquy about the need to advertise in this competitive market, something Nathan was sure they'd covered before and all agreed on.

The problem was their current campaign was tanking. They needed someone to take over. Someone who knew the market and what it would take to get GS&I's name into every household.

"Well, I think..." Dexter Ambrose interrupted Craig, and Nathan had to bite back a groan. Ambrose always began a statement with 'I think.' He was the Vice President of something or other. Nathan couldn't recall what it was the man did and his mental slip made him silently swear to himself.

"...Danielle Hollis."

Nathan's head snapped up. "What did you say?" The entire table fell silent as everyone turned to look at him. "What did you say about Danielle Hollis?" he asked.

Dexter cleared his throat and anxiously looked at his colleagues. "I was saying that it was too bad no one knew where she was. We could use her expertise for this ad campaign. Every campaign she designed has brought in millions for the company who hired her. But...uh..." He cleared his throat again. "No one knows where she is."

"What do you mean no one knows where she is?" Nathan felt as if someone had nailed his ass to the chair. He couldn't move.

Dexter shifted in his seat. Moisture began to bead on his bald head. "She worked for Taylor and Quinn out of New York and, like I said, she was the best. Everyone wanted Danielle Hollis for their ad campaigns. Then suddenly, she left T&Q. There was speculation she was going to start her own advertising firm and, believe me, it would have been a success." Dexter shrugged thin shoulders. "I was just saying someone like her could turn this campaign." He held his hands up and shrugged. "But no one knows where she is."

"I know..." *Where she is.* But he stopped himself from saying it. Maybe it was the memory of those brown eyes staring at him or the warmth of her arm against his every time he'd shifted gears that kept his mouth closed.

"You know what?" Craig asked.

Nathan cleared his throat. "I know some people in New York. I'll look into it and see if I can find her."

Nathan passed the rest of the meeting in a fog, itching to be free to research this Danielle Hollis who'd lived in New York City for a time then disappeared off the advertising community's map.

I lived in New York City for seven years. I can handle this measly street.

The Big Apple was large. A lot of people lived there. Possibly even two Danielle Hollis's.

He tapped his pencil on his notepad. So if

Accidental Love

Dani was Danielle, and she'd had a lucrative career in a very intense and competitive field, why the hell did she leave it to drive a rust-bucket and live in a ratty apartment?

And if she did give all that up, did she really want to be found?

The tedious meeting ended and he stopped at his secretary's desk on his way to his office. "Marian, get me all the information you can on a Danielle Hollis, advertising exec. Worked for Taylor and Quinn out of New York until sometime last year."

Once in his office, Nathan shrugged out of his suit coat and sat back in his leather chair. Placing his elbows on the armrests, he steepled his fingers.

Taylor and Quinn was a very conservative outfit with a stellar reputation. If Dani had worked for them, she wouldn't have gotten away with wearing flip-flops, belly button rings, and several pairs of earrings. Admittedly, the two times he'd seen her, she hadn't been dressed professionally. Yet, he couldn't picture her in power suits and carrying a briefcase either.

Nah. It couldn't be her. Had to be another Danielle Hollis. The other Danielle Hollis, the genius ad-exec, would certainly never live in the neighborhood Dani lived in.

His sense of relief was overpowering and immediate. They weren't the same two women, and now he could relax and maybe find this other Danielle Hollis, convince her GS&I needed her.

Millions of dollars Dexter had said. Yup, GS&I definitely needed Danielle Hollis.

He reached for a file on the corner of his desk and began to work through the massive pile of paperwork.

Sometime later, Marian entered and dumped

some more papers in front of him. "That's all I could find. I pulled the gossip column stuff, too, because I didn't know exactly what you were looking for."

Nathan's gaze shifted to the papers. "Thanks, Marian."

Marian perched on the edge of his desk. Now in her early sixties, she had been his father's secretary for years. Apparently, Nathan had inherited her along with the job, but didn't have to worry where her loyalty lay. It lay with the company and she'd effortlessly moved through the transition of father to son.

"I'm taking off, unless there's anything else you need," she said.

He glanced at the gold tiffany clock that had been his father's and Nathan hated but hadn't had time to replace. He was surprised to see it was well past six o'clock. "No, thanks, good night."

As Marian quietly left, he pulled the papers close and began reading. Several minutes later, he shoved them away and stared through his open office door into the darkened hallway. One of the pages slipped off the side of the desk and floated to the floor.

Marian had been thorough in her investigation. Danielle Hollis was the eighth child of Ben and Margaret Hollis, both still living. A graduate of the Ohio State University with a degree in advertising, Taylor and Quinn had immediately snatched her up, and she quickly became their golden child.

Over the course of her career, she'd bagged several large accounts, billion dollar accounts. As Dexter had said, she became the most sought after ad-exec, beginning in the East and steadily increasing her reputation until it encompassed the entire United States. She was a star in the advertising world, raking in millions for those wealthy enough to hire her. She could have written her own ticket anywhere in the world, done anything she wanted. No doubt she'd been making enough money to live in grand style.

Then one day she'd disappeared. Put her notice in and left New York with no forwarding address.

Nathan pulled the papers back and searched through them until he found a reprint of the society page from a year ago. The woman in the picture was a long way from Dani. The camera had picked up the sparkle of diamonds in her ears, around her neck and wrists. Her normally curly hair had been pulled back in some sort of twist. She was nestled in the arms of a slick looking blond man. The caption read that he was William Delaney.

Nathan sat back in his chair. What to do now? Dexter had expressed an interest in finding Danielle Hollis. Had said she was *the one* who could help with a campaign that was slowly going down the toilet. Dexter had also said no one knew where she was.

But Nathan did.

Nathan knew exactly where Danielle Hollis, ad-exec extraordinaire, was hiding.

Chapter 5

Sammy forgot to pick her up. Again.

Dani looked at the dark sky and the falling drops of rain turned silver by the parking lot lights. She blew out an exasperated breath and resigned herself to another walk home. In the rain. Damn her sister.

As if today hadn't been bad enough. She'd gone to her boss to ask for more hours, but he'd told her it was against company policy to give a non-management team member more hours than management. What a stupid rule.

So now she had to find a second job to pay for the Porsche and she doubted Nathan Gardner would accept a payment option. No matter how mind blowing that kiss had been.

Hitching her purse higher on her shoulder, she hunched over and prepared to step into the drizzle.

"Dani."

Startled, she jumped and just barely held back a squeak of surprise. Her heart hammered against her chest as she tightened her hold on her purse. Her manager's car had just turned the corner and she was alone in the parking lot. Well, not alone. Someone was behind her.

Slowly, she turned and let out a relieved breath. A few yards away, Nathan stood beside a black car, his hip leaning against the closed driver's door, arms crossed over his chest, hair slightly damp from the rain.

"I take it your sister forgot you again."

Accidental Love

Her heart went from hammer blows to flips to flutters. Recollections of that magnificent kiss raced through her, making her weak in the knees.

"Come on." He tilted his head, indicating his car. It was a different one this time. A sporty, black BMW. Another rich man's car.

"I'll take you home," he said.

No. This so wasn't a good idea. Hadn't she learned her lesson Friday night? The man kissed like an angel. Except he wasn't looking very angelic right now. He was buttoned up, as usual, in a suit coat, his tie still in place, looking like the million bucks he was reported to be worth. But this time, instead of a twinkle of a smile in his eyes, there were lines fanning out from the corners and his lips were pinched. This wasn't the Nathan Gardner who had kissed her three nights ago. This Nathan Gardner put her on edge, made her wary. Brought back all those feelings she thought she'd outrun when she'd left New York.

He watched her, his gaze solid and unwavering. As if he were evaluating, storing away information, and that made her more nervous.

"How'd you know what time I got off work?" she asked.

"I called the store. Have you eaten dinner?"

The question caught her off guard and she answered without thinking. "No."

"Neither have I. Have dinner with me?"

She hesitated.

"Please," he added. "I've had a hellish day."

Was that the reason for the tension coming at her in waves?

"Just dinner, Dani. I promise." He hadn't moved. His hip was still cocked against the car door. She'd only seen two of his cars, but the two together totaled a hell of a lot more than she'd make in the next year if she kept going in the direction she was headed. *Rich guy*, her mind whispered and her body reacted, ready to run in the opposite direction.

They're not all bad, she told that voice, but she only half believed herself.

He tilted his head. "Do you really want to walk home in the rain?"

Her stomach grumbled, reminding her that lunch had been a long time in the past and a bagel just wasn't enough to sustain a long walk home. With a resigned sigh, she climbed in.

They rode in silence, with only the occasional swipe of the wiper blades and the pitter-patter of rain on the windshield to break the quiet. Dani studied Nathan out of the corner of her eye. He drove with both hands on the wheel, not like the other night when he steered with one wrist, the other hand caressing the gearshift.

His lips—those gorgeous lips she'd nibbled on two nights ago—were pulled into a thin line and the muscles around his jaw flexed a few times.

"You okay?"

He shot her a surprised glance before turning back to the road. "Why wouldn't I be?"

She shrugged. "You just seem stressed."

"Hard day at the office."

"Ah." She left it at that and stared out her window.

"You like Italian?"

"Sure," she said, not really wanting to go to dinner with him, especially in his current mood. She needed to think about where she was going to come up with the extra money for his car repairs. Her parents? She dismissed the thought almost immediately. She'd made her decision. This was her bed to lie in. Besides, even though they'd offered countless times, they weren't exactly rolling in loose cash and neither were any of her brothers and sisters.

Nathan sighed and ran a hand through his damp hair. "I'm sorry, Dani. It really was a hellish day."

"I understand. You don't have to take me to dinner."

"No. I want to." He reached over the center console and brushed his hand against her thigh, a white-hot touch that had her clasping her knees together. Oh, God, please don't touch me. It'd never been like this with William. This spine-tingling roller coaster ride of want and need. And it scared the hell out of her. She didn't need a man in her life, especially a rich man who had the resources to expose all her secrets and destroy the peace she'd worked so hard for.

The restaurant was a tiny Italian place snuggled between an art gallery and a bead shop in an upscale neighborhood. It smelled of roasted garlic and baking bread. Immediately Dani's stomach began to clamor for sustenance. Her mouth watered as the server set a heaping basket of rich, yeasty bread before them.

The wine steward uncorked a bottle and held it out for Nathan's inspection. Nathan nodded and the man poured while Dani eyed the bread and real butter.

It'd been a long time since she'd eaten in a place like this, but not so long that she forgot her manners or which was the salad fork. She wiped her damp hands on her pants and breathed deeply to slow her hammering heart. This place brought back too many memories of similar restaurants in New York with another man, who probably ran in the same circles as Nathan.

Nathan reached for his glass of red wine and studied her, searching her face as if he were looking for something. She swallowed, almost too nervous to eat. Almost.

"When I drove you home from the bookstore the other night, you said you lived in New York. When did you leave?" he asked.

"About a year ago," she said.

"How long did you live there?"

She debated how much to tell him, what to tell him. A lot of people lived in New York, still more left New York. "Seven years."

Her hand was lying near her wine glass. He reached out, turned it palm up, and caressed her with the tip of his finger. The feather light touch sent a live arrow racing up her arm until it burned inside her. Her own gaze dropped to their hands where he continued to stroke, causing her breath to heave in her chest.

"Where did you live?" he asked.

And just like that the connection was broken, even though he still held her hand. Oh, he was good. She'd give him credit. He knew exactly how he affected her and used it to his advantage. Just like William.

She snatched her hand away, reached for a piece of bread and buttered it, aware of his gaze caressing her face, probing where he had no business probing. She should walk out, but she had no intention of forgoing the best dinner she'd had in a long time. Let him pay for it, while he tried to pry her secrets out of her.

"Manhattan," she finally answered. With an estimated population of 1.5 million in the small borough of Manhattan, she doubted Nathan could link her to her former self.

Defiantly she took a big bite of the warm,

soft bread and closed her eyes in ecstasy. "Mmmm." A crumb fell from her lips and she caught it in the palm of her other hand. "This is delicious," she said.

Table manners be damned. She'd lived too long by the rules—studied and evaluated for her performance. If Nathan Gardner didn't like that she spoke with her mouth full then he could go to hell.

However, instead of finding condemnation when she looked up, she encountered smoky eyes filled with the heat of desire. His look was like a punch to the gut, all but stealing her breath. She swallowed her rather large bite, their gazes locked on one another. Oh, my. What she saw in those blue depths was enough to make her thighs quiver.

She placed her piece of bread on her plate and Nathan broke the sexual connection by looking away.

"So," he said, "Manhattan."

Butterflies started fluttering in her stomach and she realized she'd made a grave mistake. He may not be able to link her to her former self, but he could come to other conclusions. She'd made the error of forgetting that Nathan Gardner ran a multi-billion dollar corporation. He wasn't an idiot.

"Manhattan's pretty pricey," he said.

With another offhand shrug, she took a sip of wine, hiding behind her glass, praying the waiter would arrive with their food.

"What did you do in Manhattan?"

"I..." She set the glass down carefully, thinking quickly. *Half-truths.* "Worked in advertising."

"That sounds exciting."

"It was far from exciting. I, um, ran off copies

and stuff. Did the grunt work for the big ad-execs. More like the behind-the-scenes person." Her heart beat a little harder, and could she sound any more like an idiot with all the "ums"? Of course maybe sounding like an idiot was the way to go. He'd never realize exactly what she did in advertising.

She'd loved her job. It had been exciting. The thrill of landing an account. The creative process. She didn't care what it was—widgets, refrigerators, butter—it didn't matter to her. She never felt more alive when trying to find the right idea, the right wording, that would make people decide they had to have whatever it was she was selling.

From across the table Nathan studied her, his arms folded in front of him, his hundred-dollar haircut boyishly mussed from the rain. The candlelight between them flickered over his face, casting parts in angular shadows and other parts in stark relief.

"How'd you afford a place in Manhattan working a job like that?"

She'd known it was coming. Had hoped it wouldn't, but just as certainly knew Nathan wasn't going to give up. "Is there a reason for all the questions, Mr. Gardner?"

His eyes narrowed. "Call me curious. I can't figure out why you would give up New York for the bad streets of Cincinnati. Most women I know would prefer New York."

"Then I guess I'm not like most women you know."

He lifted his glass in a salute and a wicked smile. "Touché. And thank God for that."

She leaned forward. "So tell me about your bad day. What happened?"

He hesitated, then tilted his head. Was that

a glimmer of mischief she glimpsed in his eyes or the reflection of the candlelight?

"Maybe you can help. I had a meeting with my vice-presidents. Apparently our ad campaign isn't working and we need to revamp."

From the frying pan to the fire. That's what she felt like. In an attempt to divert the conversation from her, she merely managed to pull herself right back into it. Her mouth went dry, but when she reached for her wine glass, her hand trembled and she had to quickly put it in her lap, but not before Nathan saw it.

"I doubt I can help you." But damn her traitorous mind was already working on possibilities.

"You said you work in advertising."

"Behind the scenes. And I *worked* in advertising. Past tense."

She sent a silent prayer of thanks when the server arrived with their meals. She didn't have to feign her famished state, but all the same, she concentrated on her food.

From beneath her lashes, she looked at Nathan as he swallowed a bite of lasagna. When he caught her stare, he winked and gave her a long, lazy smile, then took a sip of wine as if he hadn't just melted her bones or set her blood on fire. Or rocked her carefully constructed world.

He wasn't as tense as when they'd first arrived, but there were still shadows in his eyes and lines around his mouth. Was the advertising campaign bothering him?

She didn't want to know. She had enough of her own problems, thanks to Nathan and his expensive car. So why did her mind keep turning possibilities over in her head? Why was she coming up with and discarding several ideas she'd never get the chance to tell him?

The server took their empty plates away and Nathan poured the last of the wine into her glass.

"So what company did you work for, Dani?"

"I'm sure you haven't heard of it."

"Probably not. But I'm sure Craig has, he knows all about that kind of stuff."

"Craig?" She cooled the palm of her hand by rubbing it against the sweating glass of water.

"My Vice President of Marketing." He leaned forward, tugging her hand from the glass and threading his fingers through hers. For a moment, he stared at their entwined hands before looking back at her with hungry eyes. "Who would you recommend to help us with our advertising?"

She yanked away from him. "It's an ever-changing business, Nathan, and I've been out of it for almost a year. I couldn't begin to recommend anyone." A lie. Several names came to mind. Good people who would treat Nathan and his company right. But he couldn't go to those people with her name on his lips.

Chapter 6

He'd heard the warning in her voice. Saw the barriers slam into place, and he'd ignored it.

He knew, being the heir apparent to GS&I, people were watching him, evaluating and weighing his performance. His father had left some enormous shoes to fill. Flushing out Danielle Hollis would be a feather in Nathan's cap.

But more than wanting to acquire the ex-ad exec, more than wanting to turn this ad campaign around, more even than wanting to see approval in his old man's eyes, Nathan wanted to unearth Dani's secrets. Wanted to know why, whenever he mentioned New York, she evaded his questions.

Danielle Hollis, advertising queen bee, was his job. Dani Hollis, bookseller and car crusher, was personal. And right now, Nathan wanted to get very, very personal.

As long as he could compartmentalize, keep his private life separate from his business, he would be okay. He'd done it before, he could do it again.

They walked to his car. Considering the late hour, the parking lot was empty, his belly was full, and he had a beautiful woman beside him. A woman who intrigued him, who made his stomach muscles clench every time she looked at him with those big golden eyes.

Oh, yes, he definitely wanted this to become

personal.

The rain had stopped, leaving the pavement wet, his car glistening with silvered drops of water. Even though it was mid-September, the humidity cloaked them, making it steamy. Hot. Funny how it matched the heat inside him.

He walked her to the passenger side of the car, but surprised himself—and apparently her, because her eyes went wide—as he backed her against the door, fitting his hips neatly between hers.

He made sure to keep his erection from pressing into her. Too soon.

Taking her face between his hands, he lowered his head, brushing his lips against hers. She tasted of roasted garlic, red wine, and unbearable heat. Heat he wanted to climb into. Heat he wanted to set himself on fire with.

She pressed her flattened palms against the car while it took every bit of his self-control not to touch her everywhere else. He wanted to. God, how he wanted too. But his mind kept a running mantra. *Too soon, too soon.*

He didn't want to scare her, even though this surprising and all-consuming need scared the crap out of him. He'd never wanted a woman this badly, this desperately.

His kiss moved from her lips to her cheekbone, to her earlobe, all while he kept his hands on her face, his thumbs running lazy circles over her smooth-as-satin skin. She turned her head on a gasp, giving him better access to her throat and he greedily took what she offered.

Her hands snaked to his waist, pulling him forward until his engorged staff was nestled into her cleft. The groan she pulled from him was tortured. Who knew ecstasy could hurt so damn much.

She arched forward, sending a surge of desire through him that nearly buckled his knees. He was hanging by a thread, barely able to maintain the already tenuous hold on his self-control. If it weren't for the mantra slowly turning into a prayer for patience, he would have lost it long ago.

She kissed him back, hungry and hot, nearly as desperate as he. Her small hands roamed his hips, his back, skimming his side to settle on his chest before restlessly moving on. She touched everywhere but the one place he needed most.

In the distance a car honked, someone yelled. A door slammed. The outside world slowly began to intrude, to pull him, against his will, back to reality. With regret, he ended their kiss, but not the contact. He leaned his forehead against hers, gulping in a few mouthfuls of air in a hopeless attempt to return sanity to an insane situation.

He shouldn't want her this much. He closed his eyes, inhaled the rich scent of her perfume, something down to earth, musky. He inhaled again simply because he couldn't get enough.

He should tell her what he wanted.

No. Not yet. He couldn't tell her yet. She was hiding for a reason and the part of him that wanted to keep this personal, also wanted to help her. Keep her safe. If she was hiding from something, or someone, then she had a damn good reason.

Even if millions of dollars was riding on it.

No. What was he thinking? He needed Danielle Hollis more than he needed Dani Hollis. Didn't he? Hell, yes!

"Nathan?"

Her voice brought him back to reality with a crash and burn. He took a step back, locking his knees to keep himself steady. Never, in all the years he'd been kissing girls, had a kiss so affected him. Scared him. Terrified him.

Her lips were shining, wet with their kiss. Her eyes were big, wide, trusting. He swore to himself, foul and vicious words, and wanted to tell her not to trust him. He was the last person she should trust.

Ah, hell. He was so mixed up inside, he couldn't think straight. Not about the company. He didn't want to think about the company. This was between him and Dani and a kiss that had rocked his world.

"Come home with me," he heard himself say. The invitation hadn't been a full-fledged thought before it came tumbling out of his mouth, yet he found he couldn't retract it. Not because he didn't want to, but because it felt right.

He reached for her hand, clasped her cold fingers in his. "Come home with me," he repeated, looking deep into her eyes, seeing the trust that made him wince but also seeing the shadows he wanted to banish. He lifted her hand, kissed her knuckles, never once breaking the connection of their gaze. "Come home with me." This time it was more plea than request. More prayer than appeal.

He could see the indecision in her eyes, feel it in the way her fingers tensed inside his. He wouldn't beg, although that's what he wanted to do. He needed her. Not as a solution to his work problems. But a need so deep, so urgent, he would have done almost anything to convince her.

She hesitated and, in that small moment, it felt as if someone had gutted him with a butter knife. Too soon. Too fast. He needed to slow down. Maybe she didn't feel the same way he did.

Maybe she didn't see the connection in the same light.

"I'm sorry." He leaned forward and kissed the tip of her nose, never letting go of her hand. "I pushed too hard."

She shook her head. He brushed away a blonde curl stuck on an eyelash and tucked it behind her ear. "No. It's just..."

"Too soon."

She let out a sigh. "Nathan, I want to go home with you."

He felt a "but" coming and had a nearly uncontrollable need to hustle her into the car and get her into his bed before she could express it.

Then, in a blinding flash of inspiration, he knew what had put those shadows in her eyes and his rage was intense, fighting jealousy for domination. Known for his cool head, he wasn't normally a man possessed by his emotions.

He wondered if it was William Delaney, the man in the society column picture, who had made her wary of all men. Is that why she ran from New York and a promising career?

Unable to help himself, he caressed her cheekbone with the pad of his thumb. "You don't have to. I'll wait."

She leaned into his hand, pressing her cheek against his palm. Her eyes were still huge, the shadows still there. He cursed himself for his foolishness, for his need to pressure her into something she obviously wasn't ready for.

Her hand came up and covered his hand. "Give me time," she whispered.

He nodded, for a moment unable to speak around the lump in his throat. "What was his name, Dani? The man who hurt you so much?"

The warmth that had battled with the shadows, fled from her eyes and she dropped her hand. Quickly, she pushed away from the car, forcing him back a step.

"That's in the past," she said, turning her gaze from his.

He bit his tongue from pointing out that it may have been in the past, but it still affected her present. Tomorrow, he would take a harder look into William Delaney. If Dani refused to give him answers, he would find them on his own.

He helped her into the car, walked around, climbed in, and started the engine. They rode to her apartment in silence. His thoughts were on William Delaney and the advertising campaign, and the need to prove to a board of directors and a distant father that he was capable of the enormous responsibility they'd given him.

Dani stared out the side window, her hands folded in her lap. He wanted to reach over, grab her hand, and hold tight. So tight she wouldn't be able to let go. To run.

At her apartment, he walked her to the door, wanting one last kiss, yet knowing it was suicide to ask for it. If he kissed her again, he would ask her to come home with him again and he didn't want to push her.

He stood back and watched as she turned the key in the lock and pushed the door open. His belly tightened. He couldn't let her go, not without knowing when he'd see her again.

Placing a hand on her arm, he stopped her. She paused then turned to him, those gorgeous eyes so big and wary. "There's a charity event next Saturday night. My parents usually go, but since they're out of the country, I have to represent the family. Will you go with me?"

She hesitated and he could see the "no" forming on her lips.

"Please," he added. "I'd hate to go alone."

The "no" turned into a grin. "Somehow I doubt you go anywhere alone."

He shrugged. "Usually not. But I broke up with my..." Fiancé wasn't the right word. "The woman I'd been dating."

"Ah. So I'm a fill in."

"No. It's not like that. I'd rather go with you than Veronica." Funny, it was the first time he'd even thought about Veronica since backing out of her driveway. All his thoughts had been on Dani.

"I don't know, Nathan."

She hadn't said no. That was a good thing, right?

"Think about it."

She bit her bottom lip for a moment and Nathan held his breath. "Friday night?" she asked.

"Friday night." Then it occurred to him that maybe she didn't have anything to wear and that's why she hesitated. Damn, he should have thought of that. "Look, if you don't want to—"

"No. I do."

"You do?"

She smiled. "I do. I'll go."

"Great." He stood there for a moment, grinning like an idiot. "Great," he said again, feeling even more stupid. "I'll pick you up Friday then."

"Friday it is. And Nathan?"

"Yeah?"

"Thanks for asking me."

The moment was so sweet, so innocent, it nearly buckled his knees. "You're welcome, Dani."

Chapter 7

He lay in the dark, staring at a ceiling filled with dancing shadows, his body so hard, so tight, it wouldn't allow him a minute's peace. Let alone sleep.

With his hands stacked behind his head and his parent's house settling around him, he thought of Dani. And ached. But it was more than sexual. There was that—plenty of that. But underlying the rigid need was another need. He'd never felt this way about someone before and it scared the hell out of him. Sure, he'd thought of marriage, children, a home. The whole nine yards. After all, he'd been on the verge of proposing to Veronica.

But he'd never expected a woman to hit him right between the eyes. He sure as hell never expected a woman like Dani Hollis. She held secrets she didn't trust him with. And he didn't blame her one damn bit.

As the shadows moved across his ceiling, signaling the beginning of dawn, his thoughts switched from her firm body and wary eyes, to her secrets. And as the sun began to peek over the horizon, bathing his bedroom in shades of gray, he thought of William Delaney.

Gut instinct told him Delaney was the key to Danielle's flight and to Dani's fear.

Shoving the covers off his aching body, he padded to the connecting bedroom he'd set up as an office and turned on his computer. By the time the sun peeked through the drawn curtains, he was fully engrossed in the data flashing before him.

When it was time to shower and dress for work, he knew all there was to know about Delaney. All the public stuff anyway. The personal was a little harder to come by, but Nathan felt certain that given time, he could piece it together.

As the shower spewed hot water over his tired joints, he reviewed what he had learned.

William Delaney III was a born and bred New Yorker. Not unlike Nathan himself, the man was born to money and the heir to a multi-billion dollar business. But unlike GS&I, Delaney's business was widespread, encompassing real estate that stretched from the eastern seaboard to the western. At one point, he owned a baseball team before selling it off for an enormous profit. The man had his finger in any pie that made a profit.

He was the golden child of, not only his parents, but New York and Long Island society as well. Nathan had uncovered picture after picture of the suave, cheesy-smiled blond-haired man with actresses, singers, businesswomen, blondes, brunettes, and redheads on his arm.

For a long stretch of time, there had been pictures of him with only Danielle. Nathan thought of her as Danielle when he viewed those photos because the elegant, wide-smiled woman in the pictures was far from the Dani he knew. Gone was the hoyden with the many earrings and bracelets, the flip-flops, and baseball hat. In her place was a confident woman with upswept hair, carefully applied makeup, and diamonds in her ears.

He didn't like the woman in the pictures. She was too tense, her smile never reaching her eyes. It was as if the sleek blonde had been hiding her true self. Had she worn a ladybug belly ring beneath the ice-blue sheath in a fit of rebellion? Or had that been added later, after her flight from New York?

The captions under a few of the later photos hinted at an upcoming engagement between Delaney and Danielle. After that, there had been no more pictures.

Nathan pushed his questions to the back of his mind, refusing to give credence to the emotional vortex of jealousy that had sprung forth after reading about the engagement. In time he would discover more, like why she had considered marrying a snake charmer like Delaney and what had happened to break off their...romance? The word made his stomach turn. He preferred partnership.

Standing in front of the mirror, he tied his tie, and forced his thoughts on business. So what was he supposed to do now? He hadn't allowed his vice presidents to see it, but he was worried about a failing ad campaign that seemed to suck money down a never-ending drain. Everyone these days, from pharmaceutical companies to used car dealerships, advertised and the payoff was—could be—enormous.

After tightening the knot at his throat, he braced his hands on the dresser and closed his eyes.

That gut instinct he was so famous for told him unveiling Danielle could possibly drive Dani from him forever.

****

On his way past his secretary's desk, Nathan grabbed the stack of pink message slips and flipped through them when someone called his name. He paused and turned. Dexter hurried toward him, huffing and puffing, his comb over falling over his eyes.

"Do you have a minute?" the man asked.

Nathan nodded and, with a sweep of his hand, indicated his office door. Walking to his desk, Nathan scanned the messages, stopping at one in particular. Dani had called. As he pulled out his desk chair, he rubbed his chest above where his heart had done a massive flip. She'd called. Thank God she'd only left her first name and her phone number.

If not for the guilt eating like acid at his stomach, he would have been excited. He slipped the message under the stack and slid it to the far corner of his desk away from Dexter.

"What can I do for you?" Nathan asked as his gaze slid to the pink pieces of paper.

"I wanted to talk about our search for an advertising company."

He yanked his mind, and his gaze, back to the topic. "What about it?"

Dexter shifted. The chair creaked. "We're having a hard time finding a company who fits our needs. I can't help but think this would be right up Danielle Hollis's alley."

Nathan's jaw clenched and he had to fight to keep his hands from fisting on the top if his desk. "But you said she was out of advertising."

Dexter nodded, a thoughtful look on his face that had Nathan's insides twisting in apprehension. "What if we tried to find her?"

In a deceptively casual move, Nathan leaned back and steepled his fingers, tapping them on his chin. "Seems to me she doesn't want to be found."

Dexter shrugged. "Maybe. All we can do is ask. And if we're willing to pay enough, maybe we can entice her to return."

"But she can't be found. Even you said that."

"And you said you would put some feelers out. Talk to some buddies of yours."

Damn it. That had been before their dinner last night. Before he knew what Dani Hollis meant to him.

"No one just disappears. If she had, her family would have said something. So that tells me they know where she is."

Dropping his hands to the arms of his chair, Nathan leaned forward, suppressing the protective growl that clawed at his throat. "What are you saying, Dexter?"

In his eagerness, Dexter leaned forward too, the gleam taking on a rabid quality. "I found out she's from Cincinnati. Right here. An Ohioan through and through. Has tons of family here." He leaned back, looking pleased with himself. "I think she'd run home to family. I think she's right under our nose."

If he didn't get control of himself he was going to throw his Vice President of Marketing out the door and on his ass. Instead, he maintained what he hoped was a serene expression. "Is that right?"

Dexter nodded, a smug look on his face. Nathan played on the man's ego. "Maybe you're right. Maybe we can flush her out. Offer her enough of an incentive and I'm sure we can have her crawling to us. Eating out of our hands." He felt sick. His stomach rebelled for a terrifying moment, Nathan thought he would toss his breakfast all over Dexter.

Dexter nodded so hard his hair fell in his eyes again and he had to smooth it over his bald spot.

Nathan leaned back, tilted his head and studied the man across from him. "What do you have on her? How'd you discover she lives here?"

"Just did some checking around. With the internet, info's not hard to get these days."

Nathan narrowed his eyes, pretending to think. "All right. Good. Bring me everything you have on her. I have a feeling this needs to be handled with kid gloves."

"Oh, yes. Certainly," Dexter said.

Nathan pulled his desk chair closer to the desk and reached for his stack of messages. "Let me handle this one, Dexter. I'll find Danielle Hollis and bring her in."

Impatience, anger, and disappointment flashed across Dexter's face, but he nodded and rose from his chair. When the door to Nathan's office closed behind him, Nathan ran a hand through his hair and wiped the sweat gathering on his brow.

He'd bought himself some time. Dani's secret would stay safe for a little longer. Now he needed to decide what the hell he was going to do.

Chapter 8

The phone rang while Dani was vacuuming. She shot a glance at Sammy but her sister didn't move, her gaze glued to *The Guiding Light*. With a resigned sigh, Dani shut off the machine and snatched the cordless phone from beside her sister.

"Hello?"

"Dani?"

She stopped winding the cord around the vacuum, her heart doing a stupid little fluttering thing. A quick glance at her sister confirmed nothing could pull Sammy from the fictional town of Springfield. But to be on the safe side, Dani headed to her room and closed the door behind her.

"Hey," she said, falling backward onto the bed.

"I got your message."

She frowned at the clipped tone of his voice. "Another bad day?"

There was a pause on his end, then a sigh. She pictured him sitting behind a large desk, the phone cradled between his ear and shoulder, running a hand through his hair. "Yes. I'm sorry."

"For what? Having a bad day? We all have them."

"Have you?"

She crossed an ankle over a bent knee, studying her toe nail polish. "Have I what?"

"Ever had a bad day?"

"Several."

"So what do you do when you have a bad day?"

Word by word the warmth crept into his voice like hot milk pouring over her body. She closed her eyes and the rest of her senses until nothing but his voice cloaked her in a need that had begun beside his car the night before.

"Dani?"

Beneath the heat, lurked amusement and she opened her eyes. Good Lord, the man did things to her.

"What do I do?" Images of what she'd like to do popped into her head. Of Nathan surging over her, of warm summer breezes ruffling the curtains and two lovers beneath a full moon.

"Yes, Dani. What do you do?" His voice was low, seductive. Enchanting and entrancing. The man effortlessly wove a web of seduction, ensnaring her in his trap.

Fear churned her stomach. No! Not a trap. He wouldn't do that to her. Yet even with that sure knowledge, doubt lingered.

"Dani?" His tone went from seductive to curious.

She had to clear her throat in order to speak. "Right here."

He blew out another sigh. "Woman, you don't know what you do to me."

If it was even half of what he did to her, she knew.

"What did you need, Dani?" Now his voice was smooth as silk, friendly yet polished. Professional.

"I wondered if you were busy tonight."

This pause was longer, causing her to bite the inside of her cheek in apprehension.

"What did you have in mind?" Back to

seduction again.

"Dinner." That's all. Nothing more. She didn't tell him where though. He'd have to find out when they got there. Deep down, she knew this was a test and it wasn't fair.

Last night she'd stood on the precipice of indecision. She'd wanted to go home with him, couldn't find the words to say no to his almost desperate plea. But fear held her back. While war waged inside her—should she go...shouldn't she—he'd somehow seen the battle, what it was doing to her, and retreated.

And for the first time in over a year, the glacier that had formed around her heart had melted just a little.

"Dinner it is then," he said. "What time?"

"We'll make it early. Six. Can you pick me up since I, uh, don't have a car?"

"I look forward to it." Those five words held a world of meaning she wasn't sure she wanted to decipher. Not just yet. She'd see how dinner went. Then she'd decide about Nathan Gardner.

When they hung up, she didn't move. Just stared at her ceiling and the sunshine dancing shadows across it. Last night had been...magical. She'd finally been able to let down her guard and feel without the fear of her emotions getting trampled on. But after Nathan had dropped her off at her door, the apprehension had returned.

She squeezed her eyes closed and fisted her hands at her side. He was not William Delaney. She had to keep reminding herself of that.

Turning her head to the side, she stared out the window and the wide expanse of blue sky. She hated this. Hated what that bastard had done to her, but was determined to end it, to become the strong-willed person she'd been before William Delaney entered her life. Leaving

New York had been the first step.

Maybe Nathan Gardner would be the second.

It looked that way, anyway. He hadn't asked where they were going. Hadn't said he would pick her up and hadn't taken over her plans. He'd merely accepted her invitation and trusted where she would take them.

That was a huge plus in her book. Now, she'd have to see how he responded when she took him to her favorite place for dinner.

****

She should have known he would fit in. William had been like that. A chameleon, changing his colors to blend with the crowd. But with William, there had been disdain in his eyes, the barely concealed thought that he was better than the rest and merely gracing everyone with his presence.

Dani narrowed her eyes and peered through the dense smoke into the depths of the bar. Nathan stood at the other end, a longneck dangling from his fingers as he talked to Clint, an old high school friend of hers.

They were engrossed in their conversation as a pre-season football game blared from a TV above them. Nathan raised his bottle of beer and took a swallow, nodding at something Clint said.

His hair was in its perpetually mussed disarray. He was dressed in faded jeans that fit the contour of his tight butt. A washed-out navy T-shirt was tucked into the loose band of his frayed waist, revealing muscular biceps. His free hand rested on a cocked hip, one knee bent. No one had ever looked better or sexier. She had thought, at one time, that she had loved a man in a well-tailored suit or a tux. Now she knew how wrong she had been. So very wrong.

From behind, someone jostled her. Someone

else called out her name and a greeting. Absently she raised her arm and smiled. Nathan had been born with a silver spoon in his mouth and a multi-billion dollar business as his inheritance. Yet he stood among a crowd of blue-collar workers as easily as if he were at a black-tie affair.

When they'd arrived earlier, she'd expected a snide comment concerning her choice of eating establishments. Instead, he'd pulled her chair out and seated her, picked up the grease smeared menu, and studied it as if he were at 21.

They laughed over dripping burgers, bottled beer, and fried onion rings. By then the crowd had begun to arrive and, with bated breath, she'd introduced him to her friends. People she'd gone to school with, partied with, laughed with.

Even though for a brief period of time she'd been of his ilk, her friends had never thought of her as such, so she'd expected raised eyebrows for bringing someone of Nathan's caliber into their realm. Instead, he'd won them over. Not in the false, I-want-something-from-you way William would have, but with his friendly nature and his honesty.

That glacier called her heart melted a little more. A slow smile spread through her. He was the real thing. Something tight and oppressive began to unwind inside her, something she hadn't realized she'd been carrying around until now.

As if sensing her regard, Nathan's gaze locked with hers and he winked, then made his way toward her.

Her feet were glued to the floor. People called out to him. Men pounded his back and he stopped at each one to say something. Women eyed him speculatively, but he ignored them, while he steadily, slowly, made his way to her.

"You ready to go?" he asked when he reached her side. He took a last swig of beer and placed the empty bottle on the nearest table. His eyes weren't as distant as they had been when he'd picked her up. He seemed more relaxed. Happier.

"Only if you are."

He glanced around the bar, then back at her. "Thank you for bringing me here, Dani. I enjoyed myself."

And he meant it. By the tone of his voice, the sincerity in his eyes, she could see he truly meant it. She wanted to close her eyes and sag with relief.

William would have...

No. She refused to think of William. Not when Nathan stood beside her. It seemed wrong somehow to compare the two when there really wasn't much comparison at all.

"I hate to call it a night," he said, "but I have to be at work in the morning and so do you."

True. Yet she didn't want the evening to end. A smoky bar, bottled beer, greasy burgers, and Nathan had combined to make it one of the best nights she'd had in a long time. Maybe ever.

They walked to his car hand in hand and in companionable silence. The quiet of the night almost hurt her ears after the noise of the bar. She wasn't holding her breath, waiting for belittling words remunerating what she'd done wrong, but rather basking in the serenity of the moment. Of just being with Nathan.

He helped her into the car, walked around, and climbed into his side. A hollow feeling grew in her stomach, a need to prolong the night. She didn't want it to end just yet.

Before he could start the engine, she put a hand on his arm. "Take me home with you."

He paused, his gaze locked on the ignition where the key was half in, half out. Slowly he raised his head, the parking lot light picking out the strands of red in the brown depths of his hair.

His eyes were dark. In the shadows, she couldn't read them and she had this terrible thought that she'd said the wrong thing. She pulled her hand away and wanted to retreat back to the bar before he could chastise her, but his words stopped her.

"Are you serious?"

There wasn't a need to interpret the surprised tone of his voice. She bit her bottom lip and nodded. She'd never been more serious in her life. She wanted this, probably needed it more than she knew.

"Only if you're sure, Dani."

"I'm sure."

He stared at her for a few heart stopping moments. Moments in which her pride hung on the line, waiting for him to either stomp on it or resurrect it. She'd had it stomped on before, more times than she could count, and had survived. She wasn't so sure, however, she'd survive if Nathan was the one doing the stomping.

A slow, pirate-like grin spread across his face and he started the car. When he pulled out of the parking lot, he headed in the opposite direction of her apartment.

Chapter 9

Twenty minutes later and a world away, they drove through Nathan's neighborhood. Here was a place drug dealers didn't dare enter. Where broken streetlights didn't stand sentinel to life's poverty. Where litter didn't clog the streets or blow across the sidewalks.

Here they didn't even have sidewalks. Just endless expanses of pristine lawns and driveways longer than the dead-end street Dani lived on. Where quiet reigned day and night.

The incongruity of their two lives struck her when they pulled up to his home after driving through stately trees lining a paved drive. Regret crowded her. Not regret that she'd had, and given up, a life that someday would have provided her all this excess, but regret that she'd allowed Nathan Gardner to become such a big part of her new life.

Hadn't she walked this path before? Couldn't she, just once, learn from her mistakes?

The sleek BMW drew to a smooth stop in the circular drive and the quiet of the engine pounded inside her. For a long time, she stared out the window, at the white brick façade and the two-story pillars.

Nathan got out of the car and came around to her side, silently taking her hand and pulling her out. Apparently sensing her apprehension, he didn't give her time to dwell on it, tugging her lightly up the stone steps, through a massive front door heads taller than he, and into a dark, cavernous entryway.

She knew it was cavernous only by the echo of their footfalls.

"This is my parents' house," he said, his voice bouncing off the walls and sounding overloud in the hushed sanctity. "I've been looking for my own place, but taking advantage of theirs while they're away."

She nodded, even though he probably couldn't see her in the shadows. He kept urging her forward with a slight pressure on her fingers until they were climbing the soaring staircase and walking down a thickly carpeted hall.

Once inside another dark room, he turned on a small lamp. Just enough light so they could see each other, but left the corners shadowed.

Dani blinked and looked around. Her nerves were at the breaking point and she felt as if she were making the worse, most colossal mistake of her life. Except William held that lofty title. So, this must be her second worst mistake. Because, she feared, making love to Nathan Gardner would forever change her.

"Dani?"

She turned to him and he squeezed her fingers. His eyes were deep and dark, mirrors to his soul. And what she saw in those depths was understanding and need, and the friendly humor that seemed to be so much a part of him.

Taking her other hand in his, he backed toward an enormous four-poster bed with draping fabric secured at each poster. His gaze never left hers, his expression never changed.

He sat on the edge of the bed and pulled her between his knees, running his hands over her arms. Like bright points of flame, his eyes centered her, anchored her in the here and now. His gaze alone had the capacity to wipe away the

Accidental Love

humiliation of the past.

"Second thoughts?" he asked in a husky timber that caused her to shiver.

Was she having second thoughts? Hell yes. Second, third, and fourth. But there was also some inner strength she'd almost forgotten she possessed.

Reality check time. She wasn't in New York. The man before her wasn't William Delaney. William would have never looked at her the way Nathan was. As if she were the most treasured, wonderful person in the world. William gauged her worth not in laughs but in dollar signs.

And William wasn't here.

He was far, far away.

She had to keep reminding herself of that. Yes, Nathan inhabited the same rich, privileged world. But it wasn't the money that made a person. It was what was inside and, looking deep into Nathan's eyes, she saw nothing but kindness. No cruelty. No calculating indifference.

No. She wanted this...this whatever it was that had sprung up between them. Probably more than she'd wanted anything in her life. She sensed that making love with Nathan would be special and it'd been a whole lot of yesterdays since she'd had anything special.

So she did something she'd been afraid to do since fleeing New York and William Delaney. She took her future in her hands and shook her head. "No regrets," she whispered.

She hadn't realized how much her answer meant to him until relief flooded his expression. Yes, this was the right thing to do.

With a smile, he lay down, pulling her on top of him while his hands cupped her cheeks, his lips meeting hers in a kiss so tender, so sweet it stole her breath.

Oh, definitely this was the right thing to do.

His restrained passion touched her soul. His fingers trembled as he brushed them across her cheekbone, her jaw, the side of her neck. Each place he touched tingled in anticipation. She closed her eyes on a deep sigh, releasing, along with her breath, her reservations, her fears. Her past.

"It's just us, Dani. Just you and me in this room. Nothing else matters but us."

"Yes," she breathed. Nothing. Just she and Nathan and an entire night to get to know each other.

Slowly he rolled, tucking her beneath him, pinning her with his weight. She didn't squirm, didn't feel dominated or panicked. She felt desired, needed, wanted. Cherished.

Cherished.

Ah, how that made her feel. Like her bones had turned to jelly. Like she was the most special woman in the world.

"Touch me," he whispered in a tortured voice. "I want to feel your hands on me. All over. Please, Dani. Touch me."

Unable to deny him when he'd already given her so much, wanting to touch as much as he wanted her touch, she pulled his shirt out of his waistband and skimmed her knuckles along the warm skin.

"Ah," he growled as his eyes drifted shut. "Like that. But more."

More. Yes, more. Now that the floodgates had opened, she wanted it all. Everything. His touch everywhere.

Suddenly he sat up, pulling his knees to either side of her stomach, and in a fluid movement, ripped his shirt over his head. Her hands went to him, touching hard pectorals that flexed when her fingers dug into them, abdominals ridged with muscle, and biceps hard as forged steel.

For a moment he just sat there, head tilted back, eyes closed, arms tangled in the sleeves of his shirt as she touched and explored, studied and learned.

His skin was tanned from the summer sun. A strip of white peaked from beneath the waistband of his jeans. She ran her finger across it, almost surprised to find the pale skin as warm as the sun-darkened.

He shuddered, a tremor ran through him and vibrated into her. "Christ, Dani."

Leaning forward, she placed an open-mouthed kiss on his stomach. He growled, sloughed off his shirt, grabbed her head, and fisted his hand in her hair. When he bent forward, his abdominal muscles contracted beneath her lips. She barred her teeth and nipped.

He lifted her head and met her lips in a bruising kiss tasting of deep passion and barely controlled yearnings. Her own needs were quickly overtaking her, demanding hot, hard sex instead of the dreamy, tender sex she'd first envisioned.

With Nathan, she sensed she could let loose in a way William would never have approved of. And, oh, did she want to let loose.

He fell to his side until they lay face to face. She'd worn a denim top that zipped and he grasped the tab, slowly lowering the zipper.

His gaze followed the movement. "All night—" he licked his lips. "All night I've wanted to do this." For a moment he stopped breathing as the zipper separated, revealing bright, red lace. He groaned, pressing his forehead against her upper chest. "Christ, Christ, Christ."

The words were like a prayer. A plea for something more.

Her shirt gave way and for a long moment he did nothing but look until her nipples turned so hard she ached and arched her back to relieve the unending pressure.

"Touch me," she whispered, echoing his words.

"Oh, I will," he said, not taking his eyes off her breasts. "I will."

He ran a finger across her straining nipple and she cried out. "Please, Nathan."

A wicked grin lit his face and still he didn't look at her. "Like that, did you?"

"Yessss. More." *Oh, more. Please.*

Over the thin, scarlet lace he placed a kiss, his tongue wetting the fabric. Teeth nipped. Lips sucked until she felt her womb contract. She moaned, an animal like sound that would have startled her had she not lost her wits long ago.

He switched breasts, but placed a protective hand over the abandoned one, kneading until she writhed and gasped.

"Oh, God, oh, man. Oh, Nathan."

He gazed at her while still laving her breast. His eyes smiled and in that moment, through her hunger and craving and thirst for the physical joy he so willingly gave her, the ice around her heart cracked, then plunged, leaving the organ raw. Exposed.

For a moment she panicked, blocking Nathan's ministrations and giving reign to an all consuming, all too familiar fear. How could she have let this happen? What had she been thinking? But reality took over, and right now her reality was Nathan, on top of her, making her feel things she had never in her life felt. She abandoned the fear for the moment. Tomorrow would be plenty of time for that wicked emotion.

Chapter 10

His teeth drew on her nipple as his hands skimmed the sides of her breasts. My God. Her breasts. He'd known—okay, hoped—they'd be magnificent. Especially after seeing them in the siren red tank top the day she'd crashed into his Porsche.

Magnificent didn't even cover it.

He was sure he could probably come up with a word to describe them. If he was thinking clearly. But the moment he went horizontal, all rational thought took a back seat to pure, one-hundred percent hunger.

Hunger for the slick feel of her skin next to his. Hunger for the taste of her mouth on his, the slide of her tongue across his teeth. Along with any kind of hunger, came thirst. And oh how he thirsted for another kiss that, quite frankly, blew his world apart. Thirsted to be inside her, to slip into her wetness. To hear her scream his name. To see her come undone beneath him.

Even as these thoughts, disjointed as they were, raced through his brain at record speed, he felt her body go rigid beneath him. Lifting his gaze without pulling his mouth away from the desert he craved worse than a morning cup of coffee, he saw panic glaze her eyes.

He pulled back and stroked her sides with his fingertips. "Just us," he whispered, wondering if that stupid fuck, William Delaney had put the panic there. "Just us," he repeated, consciously making his voice soft and reassuring.

Accidental Love

His cock ached. No, ache was too mild a word. He hurt, damn it. But he made himself slow down. Kept murmuring words that didn't make sense, yet flowed out of him. Slowly, the panic receded, her body relaxed beneath him until the Dani that had kissed his stomach returned.

Biting back a sigh of relief, he kissed her, taking his time, exploring the contours, the edges, the corners of her mouth. Learning her through taste and touch.

Both hands found her breasts, found the catch nestled innocently between them. With a flick of his fingers, they spilled into his hand and he groaned, burying his face in them, inhaling the scent of Dani.

He'd go to his grave remembering that citrus smell.

He'd been right. Magnificent didn't come close to describing them. Well-rounded, they were just a little more than a handful. Exactly how he liked them. Enough to handle, but not too much. Her nipples were erect, eliciting another grown. Erect and rose-tinted. Unable to stand it any longer, he licked them, tasting their fullness, craving more.

He shifted, demanding his body be patient. His jeans were too tight, his zipper close to bursting. Christ he needed to relieve the pressure building inside him. If she didn't touch him soon, he'd go crazy.

"Touch me," he begged into her mouth. "Please, Dani. I'm begging."

So this was what it came down to. Him begging. Hell, he didn't care. Not right now at least. He'd beg. He'd damn near plead if he had to. What he wouldn't do was let go of this moment. Not for anything.

What about the advertising account? Would you give this up for Danielle Hollis's expertise? The little voice inside his head pissed him off. This was between him and Dani. There was no one else, no William Delaney, no advertising campaign. Nothing but the two of them.

Yet, try as he might, he couldn't ignore the sliver of guilt that took the edge off his clawing need. A tiny part of him refused to admit this had gone way beyond personal. That somewhere, somehow, he had crossed the line and his professional life was going to come crashing into his private.

Then Dani's hands fumbled at his belt, brushing his engorged cock, and all thought flew away. He squeezed his eyes shut, enduring her fingers as they worked his belt, as they grazed his head. Sweat broke out on his brow as he ground his teeth together. Finally, the belt gave way. Then she reached for the snap and more torture followed until he had to breathe through his nose and out through his mouth, concentrating, praying, he wouldn't embarrass himself and come right there.

The zipper was easy, happy to be free from the pressure his cock had put on it. Instantly her fingers were on him, circling him, rubbing the tip. His hips bucked, followed the rhythm she had started. And the pressure he'd thought couldn't possibly get any worse, doubled, tripled.

He was fast approaching a quick and undignified ending. In a minute he'd stop her. As he rolled to his back, her hand followed. His jeans were pushed down past his hips, her breasts, as she rose above him, swayed. He had to lick his lips to moisten a suddenly dry mouth, but for life of him couldn't take his eyes off her breasts.

Accidental Love

Then instinct took over. The end rushed forward. Without the fortitude to stop her, knowing he would embarrass himself and not give a damn, he clenched his eyes closed, grabbed fistfuls of the comforter, and prepared himself.

Everything stopped. Her hands left his pulsing cock. For a moment he simply lay there, giving his body time to calm down. Damn, that had been close. What was it about Dani Hollis that made him lose all control?

Another thought swiftly followed. He didn't care.

He cracked an eye open to find her shrugging out of her top, tossing the fuck-me red bra to the floor. With an impatient tug, she yanked on his jeans.

Shit, he was like a sixteen year old in the back of Daddy's car with his first girl. Green and horny as hell.

Deciding this was not the time to be passive, he raised himself on bent elbows in an attempt to help her off with her own jeans, but she beat him to it.

With a twinkle in her eye she stood, gloriously, wondrously, splendidly naked from the waist up. She flicked the snap of her faded jeans and they sagged around her hips. His mouth went dry. Again.

His gaze remained glued to her hands as they did magnificent things. Things he'd only imagined in wet dreams. Her fingers skimmed up her side, below her breasts. Her eyes were closed, a serene expression on her face. His cock jumped, and then, to his utter shock, grew harder. Day-am, he hadn't thought that was possible.

Up the sides of her breasts her fingers trailed, around her shoulder, back down, always skimming, never touching the actual breast.

Nathan's entire body trembled. Down, down, down, her hands went, to the waistband of her jeans. Her thumbs dipped inside. The denim slid a little lower, revealing the tops of high cut panties. Fuck-me red. What was it with this woman and red?

His breath hitched when her thumbs came forward, snagging the elastic of the panties, but then they moved upward again. Over a taut belly to the underside of her breasts. Where they stopped. He groaned in frustration.

"Touch them," he commanded, his voice raw.

Her eyes flew open in surprise, almost as if she'd forgotten he was there. They focused on him, a smile slowly spreading across her mouth. The tiny tip of her tongue came out, licked, retreated.

Christ almighty, she was killing him.

He didn't know of a better way to die.

She shook her head. "Uh-uh. These breasts are meant for your touch only, Gardner."

"Woman," he ground out between clenched teeth. But forgot what he was going to say when her thumbs hooked the jeans again and, with an erotic swish of hips that would have done a dancer proud, they fell to the floor, leaving her in nothing but high-cut red panties and a pink flush.

He didn't think he could take any more. She proved him wrong by teasing him some more, slowly lowering one side of the panties, then the other, giving him a brief, tantalizing glimpse of blonde pubic hair, and Christ Almighty, a small tattoo on her hipbone. Sweet God above, she shaved. High and tight like a good little soldier.

Suddenly his mouth was no longer dry. He managed not to drool all over himself. Barely.

Accidental Love

Her cleft was prominently exposed, glistening with her wetness. He had to close his eyes for a moment to get his body under control.

But something hit his face with a plop and, when he looked down at his stomach, there were the red panties, wet with her moisture. He could smell her essence and, with a growl, lunged forward, hooking his arm around her waist and pulling her onto the bed, rolling above her until his cock dug into her stomach.

Her eyes were glazed. Not with panic this time. A primitive satisfaction raced through him that he'd made her forget William Delaney. He'd make sure she never thought of that asshole again. Damn straight.

Because he'd been living in his parents' house, he hadn't bothered putting condoms in the nightstand drawer. Never even considered bringing a woman here until he'd met Dani. But there was one in his wallet. The wallet that was in his jeans pocket and his jeans were...where?

Frantically he searched the floor, never losing touch with Dani, half-afraid this was a wet dream and he'd wake up before the finale.

He spotted them half under the bed and with his foot pulled them out. He quickly dispensed with the wallet, the wrapper, and unfurled the condom.

Dani took it out of his hand and with slow, methodical movements that had him straining for control once again, rolled it on. Then kissed the tip of his penis.

That was the end for him. He placed himself at her entrance, reaching down to feel her heat and, Lord have mercy... He closed his eyes on a sigh. She was soaked. His finger slid in easily. Below him, she gasped.

He opened his eyes as she dug her head into

the mattress, arched her neck. Her face scrunched up as her hips pistoned against his finger, riding his hand. Entranced, he simply watched. Her breath came in tiny pants as she squirmed and bucked beneath him. Curious to see what she'd do, he inserted another finger. She rode him harder. Faster.

He gritted his teeth. Patience. He needed patience. Small whimpers burst from her, then longer, deeper cries until one long, keening wail shattered the quiet night. Grabbing his forearms, she stilled for a moment, then bore down on his hand, yelling incoherent words.

Inside, her muscles contracted around his fingers, released, contracted again. Deep inside, she quivered. He'd always wondered about vaginal quivers—or VQs as some guys called them. Now he knew.

Slowly her body relaxed. Her eyes fluttered opened, closed, opened again.

"Oh. My. Gawd," she gasped.

"Oh, honey, it's not over yet." Not by a long shot. "Ready for more?"

Looking a bit rumpled, completely satiated, and even a bit confused, she simply stared at him for a moment. Until his cock prodded her entrance. Then her thighs fell apart and finally, finally, he slid into her moisture. No, moisture wasn't the right term. Moisture meant softly falling rain. What he encountered was a veritable downpour.

He glided in until he could go no farther. Beneath him, Dani moaned.

"Oh God, Nathan. Not another one."

Oh, yeah. Another. And another after that. All night long until they were both so spent they wouldn't be able to walk, let alone get out of bed.

Oh, Lord, she was so tight. He closed his

eyes and slid out, almost all the way, before coming back for more. Slow and easy. Pure torture. Endless ecstasy.

Dani wound her legs around his waist, locked her heels above his ass and he slid in deeper. The pressure built. The need to pound into her increased. He picked up speed and, to his surprise, felt Dani rush toward another orgasm, balancing for a moment on the precipice before one more plunge took her over the side. Like she'd done with his hand, she bore down on his cock, locking him in place while her muscles milked him.

She cried out his name, her heels digging into his backside, before going limp beneath him. Another thrust, one more, then a last, final one.

The pressure built until he finally exploded. It felt as if he'd been torn in half. Never had an orgasm felt this powerful. It burst through him and he had to fight to keep from jamming himself so far into her that he would tear her apart.

He yelled out, something he'd never done before, arching his back to get as far inside her as her body would allow and still it wasn't enough. His cock pulsed, squeezing out of him every last drop until he was bled dry.

Ever so slowly, his world righted. He floated back from his high and slumped on top of her, too spent to even hold his weight off her.

"Christ almighty," he murmured into her neck.

"Tell me about it."

"There aren't enough words. At least not in my vocabulary." Finding a last reserve of energy, he disposed of the condom then flung his thigh across hers to anchor her to the bed, and pulled the comforter over the both of them.

He had to tell her. After the round of sex that had rocked his world, he had to tell her. And not because it had been the best sex of his life and he wanted more. But because he'd witnessed the panic in her eyes and while she lay beneath him, exposed to him in the most vulnerable way a woman could be, he'd fallen for her.

Love.

Could it be?

He couldn't think of any other emotion that would make him want to run out, slay her dragons, and hold her tight for fear she would disappear.

If it wasn't love he was feeling, it was damn near close.

He had to tell her.

Tonight.

After a short nap.

Chapter 11

Dani bent over, searching into the lighted interior of the biggest, industrial sized refrigerator she'd ever seen. Cold air slapped her face, but she figured she needed a cooling down after that session of lovemaking. Whoo-eee, Nathan Gardner was one super-fine lover.

Even with the refrigerated air hitting her, her face still heated in a blush. Making love to him had not only been earth shattering sensational, but it had torn apart the protective walls around her heart. Yeah, at first she'd been scared to death. But now... Now she kinda liked the feeling of not being afraid.

Maybe she could finally put William Delaney in the past where he belonged. Okay, it wasn't hell and many a night she'd consigned the bastard to hell. But the past was good. The past meant she could move on.

Move on with Nathan?

She hoped so. Oh, how she hoped so.

Something cold slithered up the back of her bare thigh, pushing the T-shirt she'd thrown on. She yelped and jumped away. The refrigerator door thumped closed right before strong hands pushed her against it, pinning her to it. Lips descended on hers in a forceful kiss that turned her knees to jelly and melted her bones.

She buried her hands in Nathan's hair, running her fingers through the tousled mess as his hands roamed beneath her shirt, eliciting little noises of pleasure deep in her throat.

He pulled away and stepped back, allowing her a full, gorgeous view of him dressed only in frayed jeans, the top button unsnapped, barely hanging on slim hips, dipping just below his belly button.

A five o'clock shadow played along his strong jawbone and dusted his cheekbones.

"I missed you in bed." His husky voice sent shivers down her spine that had nothing to do with the cold stainless steel at her back.

"You fell asleep."

A sheepish look crossed his face. "Sorry about that."

She shrugged. She didn't care that he'd fallen asleep. It had given her the opportunity to study him. Lately he seemed tense and preoccupied. Especially after coming straight from work. But in sleep, all that drained away.

His gaze went to the refrigerator at her back. Something in his eyes flared. "I can take care of you if you're hungry."

She laughed. "For food. I'm hungry for food."

"Ah." He shooed her away. She ambled toward the butcher-block kitchen table and sat in a cane-back chair feeling the scorching path of his gaze as he followed her movements.

When she was settled, he turned away, rummaged in the freezer, and came out with a gallon of ice cream. He grabbed two spoons on his way to the table and sat opposite her, prying off the frozen lid.

"Decadent," she breathed, reading the label. Chocolate, chocolate chip. Her very favorite.

"Nothing but." He dipped a spoon in, came up with a mound of the gooey stuff and fed it to her. There was something so erotic about being fed in a darkened kitchen in the middle of the night while sitting at a table wearing nothing but a T-shirt.

She closed her eyes and groaned, licking the chocolate off her lips. When she opened them, Nathan was staring at her, the dripping spoon caught in mid-air. His gaze followed the movement of her tongue as she licked her lips again. His own tongue came out, mimicking her movement.

Oh, Lord.

Shaking his head, as if he had to pull himself from some trance, he handed her the other spoon and they dug into the ice cream. For several minutes, they made no sound other than to slurp.

The scene was so homey, so comfortable. With William...

She went still, her spoon halfway to her mouth. Disgusted, she plopped it back in the carton. Hadn't she just told herself she was over William? So why would she think of him now? Why was she constantly comparing the bastard to Nathan?

"What's wrong?" Nathan stared at her, honest concern darkening his expression.

Her heart did a slow roll as she realized she couldn't exorcise William. Why? Why did he have this stranglehold on her?

She stared out the French doors to her right, to a pool lit from beneath with underwater floodlights. She rubbed her hands against her thighs, wanting to cry at the loss of comfort she'd been feeling for the past several hours.

"Dani?" Nathan reached across the table and pulled on her arm until her hand came up. He grabbed onto her, twining his fingers with hers. "Tell me."

She shook her head, unable to speak around the lump in her throat.

"Tell me," he urged. "What is it that puts the

panic in your eyes?"

Startled, she swung her gaze to his. Had she been that transparent? She wanted to laugh. All this time she thought she'd been hiding behind this bad girl image. An image William would have abhorred, and Nathan had seen right through her.

He let go of her hand and sat back. "What was his name?"

She opened her mouth, then closed it. "H-how did you know?"

His face was clear of any expression. He shrugged. "A good guess."

She nodded, accepting the explanation without looking too deep at it. "William Delaney." For a moment she couldn't believe she'd actually said his name out loud.

"What did he do?"

She lifted her shoulder and let it fall as she stared at the ice cream container. "It was more what I did."

"You?" He sounded surprised.

"Me."

"Tell me about it."

"Why?"

"Because the bastard's standing between us. Because no matter how happy you are, it always comes to this. Because I want to kick his ass and need to know where to find him."

That startled a laugh out of her. She looked at him to see one side of his mouth tilted in a smile that didn't reach his eyes. Good God, he was serious.

"You can't—"

"I know. But it makes me feel better to say it."

Oh God, she loved this man. The thought didn't surprise her. She had probably been

Accidental Love

leading up to it for a long time. He was so good. So perfect.

She had thought William was perfect too at one time.

"Dani." Nathan leaned forward, grabbed her hand once again and rubbed his thumb along her knuckles. She stared at the movement, too afraid to look at him. Afraid she'd cry. Afraid she'd spill the sorry, sick story. Afraid she'd read condemnation in his eyes.

"Dani," he repeated, then cursed. "I'm not good at this stuff."

Against her will, she looked at him. "What stuff?"

He chuckled as he continued to rub her knuckles, his eyes locked on their hands. He waved his other hand in the air as if the action said what he couldn't. When his eyes met hers, they were dark and brooding.

"You know..." He let the word trail off. "This... Relationship stuff."

Her heart skipped a beat. Relationship? Oh God, she'd hoped there was something there, but hadn't been sure. Then William's name had come up and all the humiliation she'd so far forced away returned. Now... Had he really mentioned a relationship?

He swallowed. "I, uh... Ah, hell. There's something between us, Dani. And... I want more. But, with this William guy in the way..."

"We dated," she blurted out, then sat back shocked the words had actually left her mouth. As if a floodgate had been opened, she found herself spilling the entire mortifying story.

"We met on an advertising campaign. He contacted the company I worked for and requested me."

Nathan's brows furrowed and she realized

she hadn't told him the entire story. So she started from the beginning. From the moment she graduated from Ohio State University, being hired at her dream job with Taylor & Quinn. Taking the fast track up the ranks until she was their top advertising executive. The thrill of it all. Of doing what she loved. Of not only succeeding, but making a name for herself. She'd been at the top of her game. Then William had come along.

That's when her story faltered. Nathan was still rubbing her knuckles and she concentrated on the feel of his roughened thumb on her skin. Of the combined warmth of their hands.

"So you met William Delaney."

"So I met William Delaney."

"Tell me about him."

She licked suddenly dry lips, her throat closing off any words tried to escape.

"Dani. Tell me. What happened?"

"H-he asked me out. We dated. He was..." How to describe William. He was such a complex man. Smooth, suave, sophisticated. She'd met sophisticated men in her years living in New York. Dated a few, befriended a few. "He was different than the rest," she settled on.

"How?"

She shrugged. "At first, it was the way he paid attention to me." She laughed. "That sounds shallow. But he had this way about him that made you feel special."

"If that's the case, then what went wrong?"

Everything. She hesitated, but decided it was too late to back out now. "We dated. Taylor & Quinn loved it because William kept giving us more and more accounts. He had his hand in everything and he showered the company with his wealth. They...my bosses encouraged the relationship. And at first, I was...happy with it. Then..."

The smell of melting ice cream turned her stomach and she shifted her gaze to the carton where chocolate dripped onto the table and formed a small, dark puddle.

"Then what?" Nathan asked.

"Then William asked me to move in with him. There was talk of an engagement. Marriage." Looking back, she could see the pattern. She'd missed it at the time because she'd had stars in her eyes.

"Did you love him?" Nathan's voice was strangled, but she refused to look at him. Didn't want to witness the pity.

"At first. At least I'd thought it was love. But things changed. It was so gradual. He said I was perfect for him. For his reputation. His business. He promised things to Taylor & Quinn. All my friends, my bosses, everyone thought he was wonderful. But after I moved in, things changed. He changed. It started with him suggesting what I should wear. Then he'd get angry if I got home late from work or had to leave early in the morning. He'd throw these tantrums..." She shuddered, plunged into the nightmare that had been her life. She'd lived in a constant state of fear. Afraid to answer her phone at work for fear it would be him demanding something of her. Afraid to go home in the evening.

In the privacy of their home, he would mock her. Tell her she was stupid, that she didn't know how to dress, how to behave correctly in public.

Day in and day out, he would batter her with words. Sometimes merely a look sent her spiraling into self-doubt. It finally got to the point that she couldn't make a decision without him. He'd choose her clothes in the morning, her dinner dresses in the evening. When they would have sex. How they would have sex.

At work, she could hide it. While away from him, she managed to hold onto her sense of self by a thin, quickly shredding thread. She would tell herself it wasn't that bad. She was just stressed with work, with a possible, gargantuan wedding to plan.

She had no one to turn to. No one at work understood because, to them, William Delaney was their golden boy. Their King Midas.

Her family was supportive and, if they'd known, her brothers would have been out there in a heartbeat. But she was too embarrassed to turn to them.

"He would lay on the guilt. Tell me my behavior reflected on him and his companies. He made me believe that using the wrong fork at dinner could lose him millions and my company...my career...I...would suffer."

Tears pricked the back of her eyes. "Stupid, huh? Here I was, top of my field. A college graduate. And this guy could control me so easily." A tear slipped down her cheek and she wiped it away with her free hand.

William's words came rushing back. He'd been right. She had been stupid. Not for using the wrong dinner fork, but for sticking with him when deep down she'd known it was a mistake. But by that point she couldn't figure a way out without losing everything she'd worked for.

Nathan squeezed her hand. "No, Dani. Not stupid. Manipulated. Bastards like that prey on peoples' fears, their weaknesses, and use them to their advantage."

She swiped at another tear, unable to tear her gaze from the nutrition facts on the carton of ice cream. "I'd thought I was smarter. Here I was, handling million dollar accounts during the day and going home to this monster who made me think I couldn't even pick out the right earrings to match my dress."

His hand snaked into her line of vision, touched her chin and lifted her head until their gazes locked. Held. "It's not your fault," he said. "Psychological abuse is insidious and gradual. He wore you down until that was all you heard. What else could you believe?"

She shook her head and looked away. "I let him degrade me."

"Dani?" His voice had taken on a rough edge. "Did he hurt you?" He paused. "Hit you?"

Startled, her gaze flew to his. "No! I'd like to think..." She shrugged and stared at edge of the table, running her thumbnail across it. There had been a time when she'd looked down on women who stayed in abusive relationships. Why didn't they just walk away she'd ask herself? Where was their pride?

William never laid a hand on her. She'd never felt threatened in the physical sense. And she'd like to think she would have left if she had. Still, there were times, especially in the beginning, when she'd been at her lowest, when she'd wondered.

Nathan leaned forward, over the ice cream carton, across the table, and touched his lips with hers in a gentle kiss. "He's a bastard, Dani. And you survived. How did you get away from him?"

"I just walked away." She'd finally hit rock bottom. It hadn't been one big, dramatic scene that had done it either. She just got tired of it. Her career and his businesses be damned. "I left the house for work one day, but instead of turning right, I turned left and booked a flight home. Called the ad agency when I got here and quit my job. They wanted my address to send my last paycheck, but I wouldn't give it to them. I was afraid they'd tell William." She'd walked away from everything. Left her job, her clothes, her jewelry, everything behind. Including her pride. She hadn't even accessed her bank account since arriving in Ohio.

"Does William know you're here?"

For the first six months, she'd lain awake fearing he'd appear on her parents' doorstep demanding she return. "He knows my family's here, but I don't think he'll show up. I don't think he'd want people to see him chasing after me. He's too proud."

"Are you afraid of him?"

"No. Not anymore." It had taken a long time, but she'd eventually rediscovered her grit. If he did find her, and sometimes she wished he would, he would discover a different Danielle Hollis.

"Good girl." Nathan squeezed her hand again and this time she squeezed back. As horrible as the story was. As humiliating as it felt to tell it, for the first time in over a year a weight lifted from her shoulders.

For the first time since she'd met William Delaney, she cried. Big tears that ran down her cheeks and soaked into her T-shirt. Sobs that shook her body, yet cleansed at the same time.

She didn't hear Nathan round the table, but felt him lift her and settle her on his lap. His hands rubbed her back as he tucked her head into the crook of his shoulder. He talked to her, but she couldn't make out the words through the racking sobs. It was enough to feel his voice vibrate through his chest. Enough to know he

Accidental Love

didn't pity her.

When her crying jag ended, they were both wet with her tears and she was emotionally exhausted. Nathan carried her upstairs and tucked her into his bed. She grabbed his hand as he turned to go. "Don't leave me."

He kissed her knuckles. "I won't. But I have to put the ice cream away. I'll be back."

She nodded as she drifted off to sleep. *I love you.* The words floated through the last bit of consciousness.

****

I love you.

Nathan grabbed hold of the kitchen counter and leaned forward, clenching his eyes closed. Christ, what was he going to do now?

Right before he'd walked out of the room, she'd whispered the words that had been on the tip of his tongue all night long.

I love you.

He wanted to storm out of the house and hunt down William Delaney, make him suffer as he'd made Dani suffer. The bastard had taken an intelligent, beautiful woman and turned her into an insecure person who questioned every decision.

Granted, the Dani he knew now was more self-assured, had regained some of her confidence, but he saw the uncertainty in her eyes at odd moments. The self-doubt.

Nathan smacked his palm on the counter and uttered a string of curses. What he wouldn't do to set that bastard straight. What he wouldn't do to wrap his hands around the snake's neck and squeeze.

He paced the kitchen, too restless to go upstairs, afraid he'd wake Dani when she needed to rest.

Obviously, he couldn't tell her about his advertising campaign. GS&I would have to find someone else. He'd tell Dexter he'd found Danielle and she was out of the business. Somehow he'd convince the man to quit obsessing over her.

As much as his company would benefit from her expertise, he didn't want that between them.

That decided, he cleaned up the melted ice cream and headed for Dani, content to curl his body around her and hold her all night long. He'd hold her for as long as it took to erase the shadows from her eyes.

Chapter 12

Nathan pulled her in closer, her back to his chest, and rested his chin on the top of her head. Dani liked feeling his arms around her, his strong thigh thrown over hers. They'd just finished making love again and both were content to snuggle for a bit, fading in and out of sleep occasionally, talking when the mood struck.

It was as if they'd built their own safe haven, a cocoon from the rest of the world. In a few hours, Nathan would have to get ready for work, Dani to go home. But for now, they were together and the real world far away.

"Tell me about your family."

"Hmmm." Dani stretched, and moved Nathan's hand back to her breast where he'd been cupping it. "There are six of us. I'm number three. I have one older sister, one younger sister, and three brothers."

"Like the Brady Bunch."

She smiled. "Sort of."

"Sounds like fun."

"Not at the time, but looking back I can see it was. What about you? Any brothers and sisters?"

"Nope. Just me. I was the late-in-life surprise." There was no inflection to his voice, no way for her to tell if that was a good or bad thing. "Do they know about William," he asked softly.

"They know. I had to tell them when I called from the airport with just the clothes on my back and what money I could scrounge together in my purse."

He tightened his arm around her waist and rested his chin on her shoulder. "And?"

Dani sighed. "And my brothers wanted to fly to New York and beat the crap out of William, but I wouldn't let them. My mom tried to feed me, and my dad tip-toed around me with a murderous look on his face."

"I'm sorry."

"Don't be."

They drifted off to sleep then.

****

"Tell me about Veronica," she said.

The sun was just breaking through and they hadn't slept much, but neither seemed to care. They'd talked, laughed, made love, talked some more. Slept little.

Nathan stirred. "We dated. I broke it off."

Dani grinned. So like a man to put an entire relationship into six small words. "How long did you date?"

His thumb drew lazy circles on the inside of her wrist. "A while."

"A month? Two months?"

"Two years."

She stilled and the smile slipped away. "Two years? You dated two years?" She didn't feel jealous. She didn't. Yes, she did.

Nathan drew her hair back from her neck and kissed the tender spot behind her ear. Dani shifted away. "When did you break up?"

Nathan sighed. "Friday."

Dani flipped onto her back and stared at him in disbelief. "You broke up with the woman you'd been dating for *two years* Friday night?" And jumped right into bed with *her*?

"It's not what you're thinking, Dani." He shifted to rest his head on his hand.

"What am I thinking?"

"That I jumped from her bed to yours."

"Technically, we're in your bed."

"You know what I mean."

"No, I don't."

He pressed his lips together and she could almost see him thinking, forming words. She waited. Waited to hear what he had to say. Waited to believe in him because oh how she wanted to believe in him.

"It wasn't serious."

"Two years is pretty serious."

"My father hooked us up. Veronica was perfect. For him. She had the perfect career, the perfect pedigree. She was exactly what he was looking for in my wife. But not what I was looking for."

"And it took you two years to figure this out?" Perfect pedigree. Dani most certainly did not have the perfect pedigree. Her parents were hard working, salt of the earth people, who didn't know a salad fork from a dinner fork.

"Yeah, I guess it did take me two years to figure it out. Dumb, huh?"

"No." But she wasn't really following the conversation. She was thinking of Veronica's pedigree and her career. "What'd she do?"

His brows furrowed. "What do you mean?"

"Her career. What'd she do?"

"She was a defense attorney."

And Dani was a clerk in a bookstore. Definitely not the perfect career for dear old dad.

"I know what you're thinking," Nathan said quietly.

"No, you don't."

"You're thinking you're not good enough. That you don't have the right bloodlines or whatever the hell it is my dad requires. But listen to me, Dani, my dad doesn't decide how I run my life or who I should date. I decide that."

In another lifetime, she would have had the perfect career to satisfy his father. Why couldn't she have met Nathan then? Before William?

"Stop," he said, tilting her chin up. "Stop thinking about William."

She looked away. Insecure. She hated being insecure and, no matter how many times she blamed William for that, she also blamed herself for letting him control her to that extent.

"Who broke it off?" she asked.

"I did."

"Why?"

"Because I realized she wasn't what I wanted. Because when I was with her, all I could think about was you."

She jerked away from him. "Me? You didn't know me."

One corner of his mouth kicked up in a lopsided grin. "I know. That was the hell of it. All I could do was think about the woman who'd crashed into my car. That's when I knew I was in trouble."

"Trouble?"

He leaned forward and kissed her, a tender touch of their lips. "Trouble."

Chapter 13

Nathan reached across the table and took her hand. "Go to dinner with me tonight."

After making love once again, they'd dressed as the sun was beginning to rise and Nathan had insisted they go to breakfast.

"I'm the head of the company," he'd said when she said he needed to go to work. "I can take a few hours off." She'd relented and now they sat eating breakfast at a trendy little diner.

"Dani? Go to dinner with me," he repeated.

"Aren't you tired of me yet?"

He squeezed her fingers. "Never."

"Nathan? It *is* you."

Dani looked up and froze. Veronica stood beside her, dressed in a fashionable black pantsuit, her hair swept up into a professional bun, briefcase at her side.

"Veronica." Nathan looked less than pleased, his wary gaze darting between her and Veronica, his fingers tightening on her hand when she tried to pull away.

Instinctively, Dani wanted to slouch in her seat and act as if she wasn't there.

"I've been waiting for you to call," Veronica said, a hint of censure in her voice.

"I told you not to wait, Veronica. I told you it was over."

Dani yanked her hand away, the only way she could release her fingers from Nathan's grip. This was so not a conversation she wanted to be present for. Veronica turned to her, acknowledging her presence, apparently unaffected that Nathan had just told her he wasn't calling her.

Reluctance clear in his voice, Nathan introduced them. "Veronica, this is Dani. Dani, Veronica."

"Hi." Dani smiled and tugged on her shirt. Nathan's shirt. He'd let her borrow it after she'd showered, and she'd tied it in a knot at her naval, exposing her stomach because Nathan had admitted her belly button ring turned him on. Beside Veronica's elegant, professional attire, Dani felt like a bag woman and tried to cover the belly-button ring.

Veronica smiled coolly. "It's a pleasure to meet you." Her tone indicated it was anything but a pleasure and her eyes narrowed, raking Dani with a contemptuous glare. She turned her back and faced Nathan. "Please call me, Nathan. I need to discuss something with you."

"Veronica—"

"Just call me." She walked away, toward an older man waiting by the door. Together they left the restaurant and a heavy silence fell between Nathan and Dani.

"Well." Dani fiddled with her silverware, lining the fork up precisely with the knife.

"I'm not with Veronica anymore."

"Right." Her gaze met his. "Does she know that?"

****

Nathan was yanking his tie off as he exited the elevator and made his way to his office. Breakfast had definitely not gone as he'd planned. Damn Veronica.

"Mr. Gardner—"

"Not now, Marian. Please hold my calls for the next hour." So he could think of how to

Accidental Love

breach the chasm that had opened up between he and Dani after Veronica's sudden appearance.

His assistant stood. "But, Mr. Gardner—"

"Later, Marian." He closed his office door behind him and tossed his suit coat on the small couch.

"Hello, Nathan."

Startled he stopped, then cursed. "Father. What are you doing here?"

Charles Gardner pushed away from Nathan's desk and skirted around it. Nathan fought the surge of anger that his father had waltzed into his office and made it his own. Nervously he glanced at the folders on his desk, trying to remember where he'd put the one about Dani and if his father had seen it.

"I expected you to be in Barbados," Nathan said, making his way to the chair his father just vacated.

"We came home early." Charles Gardner was dressed as if he were coming to the office for a full day's work and Nathan wondered if that was his father's plan even though he'd retired months ago.

"What brings you in?" he asked, settling in the chair and making a furtive glance through the file folders. With a sigh, he relaxed a bit. Dani's wasn't there. He remembered filing it away in a locked drawer. A drawer his father didn't have a key to.

"Wanted to see how things were going." Charles settled into the chair opposite Nathan's desk and crossed an ankle over a knee. His snow white hair was impeccably combed, his face tanned from sailing and golfing, but the sharpness was still in his eyes. A look that had built a small company into a billion dollar force to be reckoned with.

"Things are going well. You could have easily called and asked that."

Charles inclined his head, a small smile playing around his mouth. "Why are you on edge, Nathan?"

"I'm not on edge. I'm just busy." His father always did this to him; put him on the defensive with a few well-placed words.

"Busy, but you still had time to go to breakfast."

Nathan's anger nearly broke through the tightly held restraints. "You handed the business over to me, Father. Let me run it how I see fit."

"I'm still a stockholder and a member of the board."

Ah, the string that bound them. How Nathan hated that his father even had that small amount of hold over him.

"Veronica called."

Nathan wanted to close his eyes and groan, but even that small act of cowardice would show weakness. "And?"

"She said you broke it off with her."

"I did."

"Why?"

"Because I don't love her."

"She's a wonderful woman."

"I never said she wasn't."

"Perfect—"

"But not perfect for me."

His father studied him. "Something's different, Nathan. What's gotten into you?"

Dani. "Nothing. Like I said, I'm busy."

"I heard about the ad campaign."

Of course he had. And of course he'd blindside Nathan with it. "We're working on that."

"I have faith in you."

Accidental Love

Do you? The question was on the tip of his tongue, but he bit his tongue to keep the words in. Sometimes Nathan wondered. Sometimes he wondered a lot of things, like if his father really had any faith in him to run this company.

Charles Gardner stood. "I'll leave you be since you're so busy. We'll discuss this ad campaign and a few other things I have on my mind later this afternoon."

"My decision about Veronica stands, Father."

His dad walked out as if he hadn't even heard.

****

Dani's manager breezed passed as Dani stocked books. "Phone for you," she sang out.

Engrossed in her thoughts, Dani simply nodded. Over the last several days, Nathan had proven time and again he was different from William.

William had wanted a woman he could mold to his own twisted satisfaction. He wanted someone to control and he'd wanted her contacts in the advertising world to further his businesses. Nathan would never do that to her.

Even so, it wouldn't work out between them. Not after she'd met Veronica. Nathan said he didn't care what his father thought, but Dani knew differently. She could see it in his drive to succeed, to prove to his father he could handle the business. He wouldn't throw that approval away on a nobody who lived on the wrong side of the tracks and no car, let alone any immediate career goals. In every way, Veronica was perfect for Nathan. She would be the perfect hostess, the perfect dinner companion, the perfect party hostess. All those things someone in a high-powered career like Nathan's would need.

At one time, Dani could have been that

person, but something inside her had died, killed off by William and his sickness, his need to overpower her, dominate her.

She picked up the nearest phone. "This is Dani."

"Hey there, beautiful."

She smiled, despite her heavy thoughts. "Hey, you."

"How's your day going?"

She heard the clack of a keyboard as he talked, and envisioned him sitting behind a big desk, his suit coat hanging on the chair behind him, his hair mussed, the phone cradled between his ear and shoulder.

"Good. Yours?"

"That's why I'm calling." His tone went from teasing to serious and her smile faded as she clutched the phone tighter. This was it. The moment she'd been dreading since she'd come face to face with Veronica. She knew he'd eventually realize she wasn't of his ex-girlfriend's caliber.

"I'm sorry, Dani, but I won't be able to pick you up from work tonight. I have a meeting and a pile of paperwork to get through. Damn. I really wanted to go to dinner too." He *sounded* genuinely disappointed, but what did she know.

"It's okay." She tried to swallow through a throat quickly closing up.

"I'll send a car for you. I don't want you relying on your sister."

"Don't worry about it. I'll call my mom."

"Are you sure?"

She closed her eyes against the constant swirl of emotion inside her. "I'm sure."

"If she doesn't show up, call me. Oh, and don't forget the charity ball tomorrow night."

Her eyes flew open. The charity ball. She

Accidental Love

hadn't forgotten. She'd even found a dress on clearance and had used what little she'd saved to buy it, digging into the money earmarked for Nathan's Porsche. So he wasn't letting her down easy. He still wanted to take her to the ball. She smiled. "I won't. I'll see you tomorrow."

As she hung up, she had an idea and called her mom, making the arrangements as swiftly as possible.

****

Dani had worked in one of the biggest advertising firms in New York, so walking through the lobby of GS&I sent a thrill down her spine. She missed this. Big business. The hushed sanctity of millions of dollars being shuffled behind closed doors. Timing her arrival with quitting time, she hoped to blend in with the people leaving so security wouldn't stop her because she wanted to surprise Nathan.

The elevator ride to the top floor was quiet luxury and the doors opened to an opulently appointed hallway where a light shone from beneath the door on one end. Dani pushed it open and peeked in. An older woman sat at a desk, typing on the computer. Immediately, her head popped up and she frowned.

"Is Nathan in," Dani asked.

"I'm sorry, but he's in a meeting. Can I help you?"

"Oh." She was disappointed but he had, after all, told her he had a meeting. "I brought him dinner." She held up the covered dish she'd carried in. "Could you see that he gets it? And tell him Dani sent it."

The woman took the plate and placed it on the edge of her desk. "Certainly. I'm sorry you missed him."

"Yeah, me too." She turned to go and

Nathan's office door opened.

She could hear Nathan's voice and another man's deeper one right before an older gentleman exited the doorway, his face turned away from her. He had an aura of wealth and prestige about him, a person who carried authority well on straight shoulders.

When he turned around, he spotted Dani standing at the elevators and stopped to stare.

"Dani? What are you doing here?" Nathan was behind the man, and Dani turned her attention to him.

"I brought you dinner. I didn't mean to interrupt your meeting."

"No interruption," the man said, staring intently at her as if he could dissect her every thought. "I was just leaving."

Nathan's expression was pinched, his lips thinned into a straight line, and his shoulders tense. Dani looked from one to the other, into nearly identical facial features and builds. This had to be Nathan's father.

"Father, I'd like you to meet Dani. Dani this is my father, Charles Gardner."

She smiled, glad she'd changed clothes and looked a little more respectable than she had when she'd met Veronica that morning. Still, she had an attack of the butterflies in her stomach. "It's nice to meet you, Mr. Gardner."

He shook her hand, a firm shake, cool skin, calloused fingers. "Likewise, Ms... I didn't catch your last name."

"Thank you for dinner, Dani."

Dani turned to Nathan. "You're welcome. I'll let you get back to work."

"Father was just leaving. Stay while I eat. Please." The please almost seemed like a desperate plea.

"Sure," she said uneasily.

Charles Gardner nodded to his son. "Nathan. We'll talk later."

His words made Dani shiver, as if they were a threat to Nathan. But when she looked at Nathan, he was picking up the plate and peeking under the foil.

"Smells good," he said with a tight smile and she realized he had heard the threat as well.

She followed him through his office door and watched as he sat behind a big desk, the computer monitor flashing blue across half his face. Behind him stretched the skyline of Cincinnati.

His sleeves were rolled up, his tie long gone, the top two buttons of his dress shirt undone. His gaze flickered to the closed door behind her.

"Was there anyone else out there?" he asked. "Or has everyone left?"

She shrugged. "The place was dark, so I think everyone else left too, except for your assistant."

He pulled the plate toward him and ripped off the aluminum foil. Dani sat on the edge of a leather chair positioned in front of his desk as Nathan closed his eyes and breathed deep.

"Mom made it. Fried chicken, mashed potatoes, and my sister's buttermilk biscuits. She's won prizes for her biscuits." Nathan's gaze turned to her in amusement and she realized she was babbling, but couldn't seem to stop. "Your father seems nice."

He grunted. "If you consider Attila the Hun nice, then I suppose so."

"Nathan!" She bit back a laugh. "That isn't polite."

He shrugged as he bit into a biscuit.

"Bad day?"

"I've had better."

That was evident in the lines in his forehead and around his mouth. "I'm sorry."

"Come here," he said and held his hand out. "I need you right now."

Unable to refuse such an invitation and surprised at how much she needed his touch, she walked around the desk and took his hand. He scooted his chair out and pulled her down on top of him.

"God, I missed you," he said, lowering his head for a kiss. He pulled away, his hands touching her hair, her face, her lips, his hot gaze following wherever his fingers touched. "I missed you so much," he whispered.

Her head fell back as he nuzzled her neck, nipping and licking his way toward her shoulder.

"I, uh, didn't expect his," she managed to say.

He chuckled, his hands finding the hem of her shirt, lifting it until his fingers skimmed her ribs, the sides of her breasts. "Me either. Isn't it great?"

She laughed. "Oh, yes."

"I'm dying to find out what color bra you're wearing." He cupped her breasts, fingers pinching her nipples through the sheer fabric of her bra. Dani's head fell back and Nathan leaned forward to suckle on her neck.

"Uh, Nathan?" She groaned. "Your assistant... She's out..."

"Gone," mumbled against her throat. "Left for the day."

"Oh." Good.

He swung her leg up and over until she straddled him. The chair creaked and groaned, but held their combined weight. His fly brushed against the seam of her jeans.

"Blue," she breathed.

"Blue?"

"My bra. It's blue."

He sucked in a breath. "Jesus, Dani. You'll give me a heart attack one of these days."

She laughed as her hands found his dress shirt and began the slow process of sliding each button through its respective hole. She pushed it off his shoulders and pulled his undershirt up.

Needing to feel his skin next to hers, she whipped off her own T-shirt. Immediately Nathan's gaze landed on her navy blue bra trimmed with lace. His thumbs circled her nipples through the fabric and she closed her eyes, concentrating on the sensation of his roughened fingers through the material.

"Oh God, Nathan." She released the front clasp, her breasts springing into his hands. He groaned and buried his face between her breasts, his five o'clock shadow abrading the skin and making her tingle all over. She held his head to her, shoving her chest forward. Unconsciously her hips bucked against him, searching and finding his erection beneath the dress pants.

Desperate for more, her fingers undid the belt buckle, found the hook and eye, and lowered the zipper. She caressed the steely length of him through black cotton boxers. His hips arched forward and he moaned.

His hand covered hers and helped stroke him until beneath them his hips thrust forward. His breathing deepened and his eyes lost focus. She sensed his orgasm rushing forward in the rigid muscles of his shoulders and quick heavy breathing and stopped. For a moment there was silence. Neither moved. Then she lowered his boxers and his penis sprang free, hard as steel.

Slowly, she climbed off him. With a

desperate sound Nathan reached for her, but she stopped his hands and went down on her knees between his thighs. She licked the tip of him and he bucked beneath her, grabbing hold of the arms of the chair. "Christ, Dani," he gasped, then moaned when she took the entire length of him into her mouth.

She closed her eyes, listening to his gasps as he panted for breath. He fisted his hands in her hair and shoved her head onto him, forcing her to take the entire length of him.

For a long time, she worked him. Bringing him close to an orgasm, then stopping. Going fast until he could barely breathe, then slowing until he cried out for more.

When it became too much, he pulled her off and leaned down to kiss her hard. She shucked her pants, climbed on top of him. He entered her in one smooth thrust. The chair rolled back a few inches, but Dani held on as she lowered herself onto him.

Nathan grabbed her hips and helped set the rhythm, his head leaning against the back of the chair, eyes closed, jaw clenched tight.

Her orgasm didn't build, didn't start off in small waves. It hit her like a tsunami, crashing over her with such speed she was unprepared for the overwhelming swell and cried out, arching forward.

Nathan held on tighter and shoved inside one last time before he followed in her wake, pumping until there was nothing left inside him.

For a long moment, she lay slumped over him, barely able to breathe.

"That's the best dinner I've had in a long time," Nathan finally said and Dani laughed.

They righted their clothes and Dani returned to the leather chair while Nathan ate his dinner.

Accidental Love

"Thank you," he said.

"For what?"

He shrugged and took another bite of mashed potatoes. "For everything. For dinner," he winked, "the food, being here. Being you." He set his fork down and stared at her for the longest time. "I think I'm in love with you, Dani Hollis."

Their gazes locked, his honest, burning with a truth she couldn't deny even if she wanted to.

"Say something," Nathan said. "Don't leave me hanging here." He laughed, but the sound came out strangled and she realized he was almost as insecure as she.

"I'm, uh, stunned."

"Stunned how?"

"This has happened so fast—"

Regret replaced his wariness. "I rushed it. I'm sorry. I should have known to take it slow."

"No. That's not it at all. I guess I thought that after Wil—"

"He is *not* a part of this, Dani."

"I'm sorry—" Would she ever get this right? Would she ever stop bringing William up or thinking of him at the worst moment?

"Don't apologize. Never apologize for that. Just know I love you."

She came around his desk. He stood, hugged her tight, and held her close.

"What about your father?"

He pulled back to stare at her in surprise. "My father? What does he have to do with this?"

"I'm not..." She wanted to close her eyes in mortification. Didn't he see? Didn't he realize she wasn't nearly good enough for him? "I'm not like Veronica."

"Thank God for that."

"Nathan—"

"Danielle Hollis, I love *you*. My father is just going to have to accept that. I'll run his company, but he won't run my life."

No sweeter words were ever said to her and she found herself blinking back tears once again. She didn't believe him, however, not after having met the formidable Charles Gardner. She sensed the man knew what he wanted and how to get it. And if he didn't find her worthy of his son, there probably wasn't much Nathan or Dani could do about it.

There was so much between them—his father, Veronica, William—yet one thing stood out more than the rest. Her love for him. She wasn't naïve enough to believe love conquered everything, but for the moment she would give the emotion it's due. "I love you, too, Nathan Gardner."

The breath rushed out of him and he chuckled. "For a moment, I thought you were never going to say it."

She buried her nose in his shoulder and inhaled the scent of Nathan. "I'll say it as often as you like. I love you."

Chapter 14

A soft knock sounded on Nathan's bedroom door just as Nathan finished dressing. His mother poked her head in. "You decent?" she asked. When he nodded, she stepped all the way in. "You're going to the ball," she said in that soft way she had. His mother was the opposite of his father, soft compared to his hard, yet Nathan knew from experience it was his mother who controlled Charles Gardner.

"I'm going to the ball."

"With Veronica?"

He grimaced. "Not with Veronica. I told you I broke it off with her."

She sat on his bed and smoothed a wrinkle in the comforter out. "We're just surprised, Nathan. When we left, you had indicated you were going to ask her to marry you."

That had been his plan until Dani crashed into his life. No, to be honest, he hadn't been one hundred percent sure of Veronica to begin with. Dani's untimely entrance merely secured that conviction.

"I met someone else," he said, admitting to her what he wouldn't admit to his father. Although, after the way Charles Gardner had looked at Dani, Nathan figured the old man knew his intentions. And didn't like them.

"Who did you meet?"

He bent down and kissed her cheek. "Someone special."

"Do we know her?" Translation, *do we know*

her family?

"No." He turned away from her speculative look.

"But she's special."

"Very."

Carol Gardner stood and clasped his cheeks between her palms. "All I want is for you to be happy."

"I am happy."

She searched his features. "Are you?"

"Very."

"Something's not right, Nathan. What's eating at you?"

He turned away, weary of bringing her into the middle of he and his father's turbulent relationship. "Nothing."

His mother sighed. "It's your father, isn't it?"

"Among other things." It was his father, and the burden of keeping his secret from Dani. He needed to tell her he was looking for her alter ego, yet didn't know how.

His mother stepped in front of him as he tried to leave his room. "If she really makes you happy, don't worry about your father. He'll come around."

He hoped so, because Nathan was beginning to have thoughts of keeping Dani around for a long time. Forever, if he could.

****

Promptly at seven, Nathan knocked on Dani's door. He tugged on the lapels of his tailor made tux. If there'd been a mirror in front of him, he wouldn't have been at all surprised to see a smug smile on his face. His mother made him feel as if things would be all right. Rarely could Charles Gardner withstand an assault from his wife. Rarely did he try. With Carol on his side, Nathan knew he'd won half the battle.

Yes, things were looking good.

Movement on the other side of the door had him wondering what outrageous outfit Dani had chosen to wear tonight. Leather? A little lace beneath it? Would she bare her ladybug belly button ring? He almost chuckled at the thought of walking into the stuffy charity ball with her on his arm. It'd do those old stodgies good to be shaken up.

When she opened the door, his smile faltered. His gaze started at the toes of her black silk stilettos and slithered up a slinky black evening gown. No way would he have to wonder what color bra or panties she was wearing because she wasn't wearing any.

Lord have mercy.

He licked dry lips as his gaze wandered over breasts freed from the constraints of a bra to bare shoulders. It wasn't that the dress was indecent, far from it.

He stopped at her face. Gone were the three pairs of earrings, replaced with an exquisite set of diamond studs. As if sensing his thoughts, her hands went to her ears, her fingers fiddling with the jewelry.

"I bought these with my first paycheck. When I knew I was leaving William, I wore them. They're the only thing that made it out of the relationship."

He nodded, not trusting himself to speak. Her normally wild hair, curls he loved to sift his fingers through, were tamed and pulled back into a twist at her nape.

And her face. He swallowed. Her eyes were shadowed and smoky, giving her an alluring, sensuous look. Her lips were a bright, shiny strawberry color, her cheeks rosy and flawless.

Overall, the impression was of

sophistication. Elegance. Class, grace, and style.

Nathan hated it.

Where was the Dani he knew? The whirlwind who'd wrecked his car, then proceeded to crash through his life. Where was the woman who wore a ladybug tattoo and belly button rings and so many bracelets you heard her coming a block away? Where was the woman who drank beer from a bottle and felt right at home in a smoky bar crowded with sweaty men?

Standing before him was Danielle Hollis, advertising executive, and this new woman scared the hell out of him. "You said we were going to a charity ball, right?" Dani's arms came around her middle, hugging herself tightly.

"Yes." His eyes took one more tour of her body. You're...beautiful." And she was. In an untouchable way.

Her smile seemed forced. "Thank you. I'm..." She waved her hand in the air and he noticed her fingernails were painted a scarlet red that reminded him of Veronica. "I'm not very good at these things."

He tore his gaze from her nails to see the uncertainty, the insecurity lurking in her amber eyes. "That's William talking."

She looked away, licked those strawberry lips.

"Dani. He's not here tonight. It's just you and me."

She laughed, but the sound was strained. "You, me, and a ballroom full of people." He heard her unspoken words as if he read her mind. *A room full of people watching me make mistakes. Judging me.*

"Come on, beautiful." He held out his hand. "Let's go wow them."

Dani hesitated. He held his breath, waiting

Accidental Love

to see if she would take his hand or slam the door in his face in fear. She may not look like the Dani Hollis he knew, but beneath the face paint and elegant dress, lurked the lady who loved ladybugs.

Tentatively, she reached out and placed cold fingers in his palm. He curled his hand around hers and gently tugged her forward to place a kiss on the tip of her nose. He wanted to kiss her full on the mouth, but was afraid he'd ruin her makeup.

On the drive over, Dani fidgeted with her small purse, opening and closing the clasp with a harsh click while she stared out the window. Nathan was known as a genius in the business world, a trait he inherited from his father, but like all men, he didn't understand women to save his life. He was beginning to suspect that all the glamour and glitz coming from Dani had something to do with Veronica. Was she comparing herself to his old girlfriend? Trying to remake herself into Veronica's image? God, he hoped not.

"I have a confession to make," she said into the silence, startling him from his thoughts.

"Yes?" He kept his eyes on the road for fear he wouldn't be able to stop staring at her, probing beneath the slick glamour, searching for the woman he'd fallen in love with.

"I don't have insurance."

He laughed out loud because it was the last thing he'd expected to hear. "I know."

She finally turned to him, her eyes wide. "You do?"

He nodded and reached over to grab her hand. "I figured that out almost immediately."

"And you're not mad?"

"No. Well, maybe at first I was."

She blew out a breath. "Oh my, God. All this time I was afraid to say anything and you knew."

They both laughed and while it didn't break the tension, it eased it somewhat.

"I'll pay you for the damages."

"You don't have to do that, Dani. The car's already fixed."

"But it was my fault. I turned in front of you."

"I was in a hurry as well. I should have been paying better attention."

"I don't know." She bit her bottom lip.

He squeezed her hand. "Dani. I love you. I know you find that hard to believe, but I do. I'm damn glad you turned in front of me because I would never have met you if you hadn't. Consider it a gift to me."

He was relieved to see her smile, a hint of the Dani he knew returning.

"An expensive gift," she said.

"But well worth it."

****

As soon as they walked into the ballroom, they ran into Nathan's father. Dani could feel Nathan stiffen as he took a half step in front of her. She edged around him, not willing to let Charles Gardner intimidate her. She'd had enough of intimidating men. Besides, she sensed that with Charles, weak women were a liability.

"Father."

"Nathan." Charles's gaze sought hers and she stared back, smiling, refusing to let him bully her.

"Mr. Gardner, it's a pleasure seeing you again."

He inclined his head with a slight smile. "Likewise, Dani. I hear you work in a bookstore."

Nathan shifted. "Father—"

"I do, Mr. Gardner. I love books."

"Good. Good." Silence fell between the three of them and to her surprise, Dani found she drew strength from that silence, from unnerving Charles Gardner. Probably not many had done that before.

Nathan took her elbow and steered her around his father, his face set, jaw muscles clenched. Dani smiled at Charles. "Have a good evening, sir."

His gaze followed her, his suspicious expression turning to something else, something close to approval, but Dani wasn't sure she was ready believe it was that easy to win Nathan's father over.

"Ignore him," Nathan said tightly.

"He's not so bad," she said, surprised she spoke the truth. Charles Gardner really wasn't that bad. He wanted what was best for his son and his company. Probably the company first and the son second and, more than likely, he thought what was best for the company was for Nathan to marry Veronica. But she'd made a step in the right direction when she'd managed to alter his original perception of her with her armor of formal wear and makeup. She'd seen his surprise and he now knew she could fit in, at least where her dress and looks were concerned, and maybe even her manners. Her job, however, was another story, but there wasn't much she could do about that.

Score one for Dani, zero for Charles.

****

Dani took a sip of her wine. Across the crowded ballroom, she caught glimpses of Nathan talking to a trio of men. All evening men had sought him out. He'd been cordial and courteous, introducing her to so many people she'd never remember their names. They'd talked mainly stocks and bonds and, eventually, she had wondered off on her own.

After the confrontation with Nathan's father, it hadn't been hard to slip into her Danielle Hollis persona and it hadn't been as painful as she'd thought. In wanting to impress Nathan—and his father—she'd rediscovered a world she'd surprisingly missed. Before William and his insidious evil, she'd enjoyed nights such as this, glamorous people dressed in elegant clothing, hobnobbing and brown nosing. She got a kick out of the superficiality of it all, but she knew beneath the shallow exterior, million dollar deals were brokered and broken. Alliances made and dissolved. Affairs started and ended.

"Hello."

Dani pulled her gaze from Nathan and found Veronica standing in front of her looking stunning in a navy beaded gown that dipped low enough to show the sides of her breasts and was tight enough to inform everyone present she didn't have an ounce of fat.

"Hello," Dani said.

"Dani, right?" The woman's eyes were cold, calculating. Dani had seen the look when she'd been with William. Other women had wanted William for his wealth, his pedigree, his connections, and were willing to do what it took to eliminate any competition. Veronica was the same, it seemed, only this time Nathan was the spoils of war.

"Right. It's nice to see you again, Victoria."

The woman's eyes narrowed at the direct hit. "Veronica," she corrected.

"Right." Dani took a sip of her wine and looked around the room, as if she were bored.

"I don't recall Nathan mentioning your last

name," Veronica said, shifting slightly so the candles and lights reflected off the spangles of her dress.

"Hollis."

The woman scrunched her brows as if she were thinking hard and Dani wanted to tell her she'd get premature lines if she did that too much, but bit her tongue.

"I'm not acquainted with any Hollis's. Are you new to the area?"

Direct hit from Veronica. She oh so nicely informed Dani that her family was not of Veronica's caliber. Unworthy of her notice. "Lived here all my life," she said. "Except for a short stint in New York."

"And what do you do?" Veronica lifted a glass of champagne from a passing waiter's tray and took a sip, her gaze locking with Dani's, daring.

"I work in a bookstore."

A look of distaste crossed her face.

"Is the champagne not to your liking?" *Or am I not to your liking?*

"No," she lowered her glass. "It's fine. Vintage, as always. The Harrington's know how to throw a superb ball."

Hit two.

"I wouldn't know. This is my first."

"Of course it is." Veronica's direct gaze assessed Dani, taking in her gown, her shoes, landing on her very expensive earrings. Dani could almost hear her thoughts. The dress wasn't designer, but the earrings were definitely real. She could see the tiny wheels turning in Veronica's mind trying to fit all the puzzle pieces together.

"Veronica." Charles Gardner swept Veronica up in an exuberant hug. With a smug smile in Dani's direction, Veronica returned the embrace.

"Charles. It's so good to see you. How was Barbados?"

"Fabulous," Nathan's father said.

It seemed Veronica won this battle. She had an "in" Dani didn't—the approval of Nathan's father. Someone brushed against Dani's arm as she watched the exchange and she looked over at a tall woman with Nathan's brown hair and eyes.

"You must be, Dani," the woman said with the first genuine smile Dani had seen all evening.

"I am."

The woman held out her hand. "Carol Gardner, Nathan's mother."

"It's nice to meet you, Mrs. Gardner."

"Call me Carol." She watched Dani with a speculative look, but Dani didn't feel like a butterfly pinned to a board like she had with Nathan's father. Mrs. Gardner, Carol, seemed more curious than condescending and Dani wondered just how much Nathan told his mother about her.

Carol opened her mouth to say something, but an older woman snagged her elbow and the two hugged, drifting away, deep in conversation. Veronica and Charles had joined another group and Dani was left standing alone, wondering what exactly had just happened.

Someone bumped her from behind and she had to hold out her wine glass to keep from spilling it all over her.

"Excuse me," the gentleman said.

The man steadied her by putting a hand beneath her elbow as he held out his other hand. "Dexter Ambrose. I saw you arrive with Nathan Gardner." He looked at her expectantly and she took his hand.

"It's nice to meet you," she said. "I'm

Danielle Hollis."

****

Nathan searched the crowd, trying to catch a glimpse of Dani in the crush of people. He'd told her he'd only be gone a minute, but an influential client had wanted to speak to him and he'd been away from her a lot longer than he'd intended or wanted.

He skirted the perimeter of the large room, easily deflecting people as they tried to stop him. Finally, he spotted her in the corner talking to someone and headed toward her.

"Nathan. There you are." Veronica stepped in front of him and reluctantly, Nathan halted.

"Veronica."

"It almost seems as if you're avoiding me."

Probably because I am. "I'm with someone tonight, Veronica."

"Yes, I saw." She pursed her lips as if even the thought of Dani tasted sour.

It angered Nathan that he hadn't seen this prejudice in her before. But then, hadn't he been the same way? Hadn't he thought the worse when he saw the car Dani had been driving?

"Have you come to your senses?" she asked, apparently dismissing Dani as nothing more than something to be stepped over.

"If you're speaking of our relationship, then no, and I won't. I'm with Dani now."

Something flashed in Veronica's eyes. Disappointment or hurt? More likely disappointment. It wouldn't harm her career to be married to a Gardner.

"We're much better together," she said, snapping the last of his hold on his anger.

"It's over, Veronica. Over. Please accept that and move on."

She stared at him for a moment with a

calculating expression and he stared back, hard and implacable.

"I do believe you're serious," she finally said.

"Deadly serious."

Her chin lifted. "Then I wish you the best."

And just like that it was over for her. No tears, no regrets. Time to move on. Nathan shook his head as she walked away, wondering how he could have even considered tying himself forever to a cold fish like Veronica. Of course, she hadn't been cold while they'd been dating. What a good actress she'd been then.

Once again, Nathan searched the crowded ballroom for Dani and found her still talking to the same man. He made his way toward her, his steps faltering then stopping when he saw who she was talking to.

Someone bumped into him, but he barely heard their irritated apology.

They were deep in conversation, Dexter and Dani. Yet it seemed Dexter was doing all the talking, Dani nodding at intervals.

Never once had Nathan considered that Dexter would be at the charity function. But, if he'd thought about it—and face it, he hadn't been doing much thinking these last few days—he would have realized Dexter's social climbing wife would have made sure they were on the guest list.

He swallowed, his mouth so dry it almost hurt. His heart beat an irregular rhythm and he rubbed his chest, trying to ease the sudden constriction.

Dexter, his face animated, was gesturing with one hand while the other held Dani prisoner by the elbow. She had to lean back in order to avoid being hit by his wine glass. Her smile was forced, her chin held high.

Nathan strode as swiftly as he could toward them, dodging waiters laden with trays of food and drink, women in sequined gowns, and men who tried to flag him down. He muttered hasty apologies to people whose feet he trampled.

When he reached Dani's side, Dexter beamed at him and looked like the cat that swallowed the canary. "Nathan, why didn't you tell us you'd found the elusive Danielle Hollis?" Dexter turned back to Dani. "For weeks I've been telling him we needed to hire you for our advertising needs. Your reputation is outstanding. And this dog—" he slapped Nathan on the back, "—he said not to worry about it. Said he'd find you himself. And here you are." Dexter shook his head as if the joke were on him.

Nearly sick to his stomach, Nathan put his hand under Dani's elbow, irrationally believing if he touched her, everything would be all right. She moved away.

"I've been telling her the advertising problems we've had," Dexter said. "Trying to pick her brain so to speak."

"I don't think this is the time or the place, Dexter." Again, Nathan tried to latch on to her and again she easily avoided him. She pierced him with those golden eyes filled with pain, betrayal, and fury.

Nathan clenched his jaw and felt his own anger rising. Anger at Dexter, anger at himself for letting this go far too long.

"Dani—"

"If you two will excuse me." She set her wine glass very carefully on the table next to her, every movement precise, as if she and the wine glass would shatter if she weren't very, very careful.

Dexter grabbed hold of Nathan's arm as

Dani slipped away. "You sly dog. You knew all along where she was. Great idea bringing her to this shindig. Wine and dine her, slowly bring her to our side. I should never have doubted you, Nathan. I should have known you would do all you could for the company. Old man Gardner will be proud."

Nathan jerked his arm away and turned, intent on finding Dani to explain. Instead, he froze in mid-step. She stood behind him, tears glistening in her eyes.

She turned on her heel and disappeared into the crowd.

"Dani, wait." He went after her, ignoring Dexter and pushing people out of his way. She made a dignified exit through the crowd, her head held high.

He caught up with her in the lobby as she headed toward the doors and grabbed her by the arm. "It's not what you think. Let me explain."

She held up a hand and any words he might have said died on his lips. Her nose was red and her body trembled. He wanted to put his arms around her, wanted to turn the clock back twenty-four hours. He wished to God he'd done so many things differently.

"How long have you known?" she asked.

He hesitated, but the time for lies was over. "Almost from the beginning."

She nodded and looked away. "I thought..." She swallowed and her bottom lip trembled. "I thought you were different, that I could trust you. I thought..." Her voice trailed off and she shook her head again. The tears brimming in her eyes began to overflow. "I thought my heart couldn't break any more than it had."

"It's not what you think," he whispered.

She looked toward the doors of the lobby

where uniformed doormen stood outside. "I have to go. Please don't follow me."

Even though it killed him, he watched her walk away. She didn't even stop. Didn't look over her shoulder. Didn't hesitate. Just walked away with grace and dignity.

Nathan approached a doorman and pushed money into his hand. "Find a taxi for her. Tell him to take her wherever she wants to go."

Chapter 15

Nathan was scared out of his mind. Dani had pulled another disappearing act and dropped off the face of the earth. Saturday morning he'd called her home and got no answer. Then he'd called the bookstore only to be informed Dani Hollis no longer worked there.

Saturday dragged on, the clock ticking away the minutes as he paced his bedroom. But the bittersweet memories of him and Dani entangled in his sheets, the sighs of their lovemaking reverberating in the mush that had become his mind, and the whispers of late night conversations, had him fleeing that particular room. The kitchen was no better because that was the room they'd been in when she'd decided to trust him.And look what he'd done with that trust?

His newly repaired Porsche reminded him of how they met, so he abandoned it for the black BMW Z4. But that only reminded him that Dani had no car. And where the hell was she anyway?

He'd practically worn out the speed dial on his phone, but still no one answered at her apartment. Where was her sister? Had the entire Hollis family disappeared? Or had they closed ranks around their own?

He considered going to her parents' house. He'd never met them but imagined, through Dani's stories, he wouldn't be welcome. Not after he'd hurt her so badly.

To flee the memories in his parents home, he

went to work on Sunday under the irrational assumption he'd get something accomplished other than berating himself and worrying.

He took one look at his desk chair, turned, and stomped out.

The nights were pure torture, lying in his bed with the scent of Dani still on the sheets, wondering where she was. What she was thinking?

And how he could make it all right?

If he were any sort of man, he'd go after her. He'd storm over to her apartment and bang on her door until she either opened it or called the police.

Early Sunday morning, before the *Cincinnati Enquirer* even landed in the driveway, he did just that. Not the pounding part, but the storming part.

He sat in his car and stared up at the darkened windows of her apartment. By the time late morning rolled around, it was apparent no one was there so he drove off, frustrated, and angry.

She'd said she loved him, damn it. Had it meant nothing? Sure, he knew her past, but by now she should have realized he was nothing like William Delaney.

Or was he? He'd wanted to use her to fix his company. But that was before he'd had a chance to know her. Before he fell in love with her. Did it matter? All she would see was the betrayal and compare that to Delaney.

If only she'd given him a chance to explain.

Yeah, and what would you say, big boy? That you really had intended to use her?

No, he would tell her he loved her. That he'd give up his company if that's what it took to convince her. That nothing was more important than her.

When he arrived back home, his parents were in the dining room, his father reading the Sunday paper, his mother working on a Sudoku puzzle. Both looked up when he entered, both put their papers down.

"Nathan?" His mother's tense voice had him slumping in the chair.

"I screwed up," he said on a strangled breath. And he told them everything. Everything. From the moment Dani crashed into his Porsche to the moment she walked out of the ball. Except for the lovemaking. There was only so much a son, even as old as he, could tell his parents.

"Oh, Nathan." His mother had tears in her eyes and his father shook his head muttering, "Danielle Hollis. I knew there was something about that girl."

Of course now his father would approve, after he discovered Dani was one of the top advertising executives in the country, but Nathan couldn't think of that now. After he found Dani, after he fixed things with her, he'd worry about his father.

In the end, there was nothing his parents could do. Dani Hollis had disappeared.

****

Dani *wanted* to disappear, but the best she could manage was to huddle under her comforter in her old bed in her parents' house. She never knew a betrayal like this could hurt physically. Only with hindsight did she realize the pain William had inflicted had merely pierced her pride. This was different. Nathan's betrayal, his lies, his playacting, had cut deep into her soul.

Beneath the warm comforter, she snorted in derision. And here she'd told herself Nathan was nothing like William. Oh, but men were all alike. He'd used her for her connections, just as William had, but she had to hand it to Nathan, he was a much better manipulator than William could ever be. Instead of bullying and preying on her weaknesses, he'd used seduction and warmth. Understanding and compassion.

To think she'd told him everything. He must be laughing now.

She wiped a tear that had slithered down her cheek. No, he wasn't laughing. She got the last laugh because there was no way in hell she was helping him now. No. Way. In *hell*. His company could go bankrupt and she'd laugh in his face. That's what he got for using her.

A sob came from deep within her, shaking the bed. Yup, that's what he got all right. And what did she get? A broken heart, that's what.

You sly dog. You knew all along where she was. Dexter's words, spoken to Nathan, made her nauseous. What a fool she'd been to think she was more to Nathan. She fisted the sheets and sobbed again. What a fool.

I should have known you would do all you could for the company. Old man Gardner will be proud. She found it hard to believe Nathan wanted the approval of his father so much that he'd hurt her in this way, but then, she'd never made the best choices in men and hadn't William taught her all was fair in love and business?

The covers were suddenly yanked off the bed and she blinked in the bright light. Her mother stood with hands on hips, glaring at her. Dani lunged for the end of the blanket, intent on covering herself up. Content with hiding from the world.

"Oh, no you don't, Danielle Hollis. I've had about enough of this."

Dani sniffed and curled into a ball, hugging Bear, her favorite stuffed animal, close to her.

The mattress tilted as her mother sat on it. "Dani, you need to snap out of this."

She sniffed again. She'd shown up at her parents' house still in the dress she'd worn to the ball, shoes in her hand, tears in her eyes. They'd taken her in, like they always did, and surrounded her with love. Obviously the coddling was over.

"Why do I always pick losers?

Her mother huffed. She never had been one to molly coddle. "Nathan Gardner isn't a loser."

Dani's head shot up and she narrowed her eyes. This was a new tactic. Usually her mother, at least, agreed that the men she'd chosen were losers. "You've never met him."

"But you've told me all about him. Know what I think, Danielle?"

"No." And she didn't want to, either.

"I think Nathan got himself into a bit of a pickle and didn't know how to get out of it. I think his intentions were in the right spot."

Her mother was siding with *Nathan*? "He lied to me."

"We all lie, honey. I'm not saying its right. I'm just saying it happens. And usually, we're sorry."

Dani wanted to cover her ears, didn't want to think of Nathan as being sorry even as his tortured expression refused to leave her memory. Had that been genuine regret in his eyes?

Sheryl Hollis took her daughter's hands and held them tight. "William Delaney was an ass," she said, causing Dani to smile for the first time in days. "He was cruel and vindictive. He hurt you in ways I can't even comprehend. You got away from him and, for that, I am deeply proud of you. Most women wouldn't have the guts to do what you did. But, honey, he still has a hold on you."

Her mother lifted her chin so Dani had to look at her through a haze of tears.

"You're stronger than that, Danielle. Don't let this man rule your life. Don't let William Delaney color your thoughts on other men. Nathan lied. That was wrong. But at least let him explain."

Dani shook her head. She never wanted to talk to Nathan again.

"You're better than this, Dani. You're the smartest of the Hollis bunch, though don't tell your brothers and sisters I said that. Use the brain God gave you. If you won't talk to the poor man, then at least do something with your life besides hide in your room."

She left, leaving the door open, her words hanging in the air.

Chapter 16

By Monday morning, Nathan was in bad shape and in no mood to face Marian or the damn desk chair. It was only the vague thought that people counted on him that had his butt in the chair. A chair that brought so many sharp memories, he nearly groaned aloud.

Forcing those memories away, he concentrated on work, snarling at people who had the misfortune to speak to him.

Then he looked up and found Dexter on the other side of his desk. It took all Nathan's self-control not to reach across the mahogany expanse and wrap his hands around his vice president's neck.

It wasn't Dexter's fault. Nathan took a deep breath and kept repeating that. It wasn't Dexter's fault.

It was *his* fault, damn it.

His fault for not telling her. His fault for not walking away when he realized what exposing her would do.

"Yes, Dexter? What can I do for you?" He had to speak through clenched teeth. Dexter's presence only reminded him that the last time he saw Dani, she'd had tears on her cheeks and murder in her eyes.

"Just wanted to update you," Dexter said.

Nathan threw down his pen and pinched the bridge of his nose. A massive headache slumbered just beneath his eyeballs, ready to burst forth. "Update me on what?"

"Danielle Hollis."

Nathan's head shot up and he pierced Dexter with a fierce scowl. "Danielle Hollis?"

"I put her in the empty office down the hall. She's all settled in, even had a short meeting with a few of us this afternoon." Dexter shook his head, admiration and something close to hero worship in his eyes.

"Dani— uh, Danielle? Is here?"

Dexter looked confused. "She said you knew all about it. That the two of you discussed her employment. Said you even hammered out her salary."

Nathan nearly choked and had to cough to hide his reaction. Salary? He wanted to groan, but was too impressed with the balls of steel his little ladybug lover seemed to have sprouted. "And just what was the salary she said we agreed upon?"

Dexter named a figure that really did make Nathan choke. *Holy hell*. This was one pissed off woman who decided to declare war with his budget. But, if everything Dexter had said and all the research Nathan had done was correct, she would be worth it.

So, what to do now? How to handle his newest employee?

For the first time in sixty-eight hours and twenty-two minutes, ever since Dani walked out of the charity function, Nathan felt a spurt of hope. Cool logic flowed through him, pushing away the panic that had fogged his brain for the past two and a half days.

He reached over and buzzed his assistant. "Marian, please tell Danielle Hollis I'd like to speak with her."

"Yes, sir," came the reply, but as Dexter was leaving, Marian stuck her head in the doorway.

"Um, Ms. Hollis said she's busy at the moment."

Nathan blinked. Marian tried to hide a small smile.

"She what?" he asked.

"She, uh, said she was busy."

Marian retreated, leaving Nathan to stare at the door. It didn't take long for him to come to a swift decision. By God, if she wouldn't come to him, he'd go to her. He was the President of this damn corporation, after all.

Still, he had to halt outside her closed door to gather his composure and prepare himself to see her again. She may have wormed her way into his company and convinced his payroll department to pay her an absurd salary, but he hadn't forgotten he'd hurt her.

Not wanting to give her time to prepare for him, he knocked on the door at the same time he turned the knob and stepped in. The sight of her nearly ripped the breath from his lungs. For the past two days, he'd been torn apart with worry and now here she was, in his building, wearing a dark gray suit, her hair pulled back. Danielle Hollis, ad-exec, in full battle mode.

She did a double take and the binder she'd been holding slipped from her grasp. She caught it in time and hugged it close to her chest.

"Dani." He cleared his throat.

"Mr. Gardner." Her tone was clipped, cold.

"We need to talk."

She placed the binder on the desk and began stacking papers, not looking at him. "Give me a few days to get settled in and meet with my staff. By then, I'll have some idea of where we need to go with this campaign."

"That's not what I meant, Dani."

"I'd prefer you call me Danielle. Or Ms. Hollis." She finally looked up at him, all emotion

Accidental Love

stripped from her usually expressive face. "You got what you wanted, Nathan. I'm here. I'm working for you."

"This isn't how I wanted it."

She tilted her head, anger flaring deep in her eyes. "What? You expected us to continue our affair while I worked for you? I'm not like that."

"No." Shit, she was good at manipulating his words, and he was just nervous enough that he couldn't say what he really wanted to say.

She looked away. "I didn't think so."

"Dani, please. Let me take you out to dinner. Let me explain."

A sad smile twisted her mouth. "I don't think so." She rounded her desk and brushed past him. It took every bit of his self-control not to reach for her. She opened the office door, clearly indicating their short meeting was over. "Like I said, give me a few days to get settled and we'll talk about where to go from here. With the campaign."

Nathan stared at her for several long seconds, anger boiling just below the surface. Obviously, she wasn't giving an inch, and wouldn't allow him to explain. She wanted to keep their relationship professional but he'd passed professional long ago. He'd play her game. For now.

He left the office, deliberately avoiding any contact with her.

****

Dani leaned against the closed office door and blew out a breath of relief. She knew she'd pushed him, could see his anger, but damn it, she was *not* going to talk about what a fool she'd been. Was not going to stand here and listen to him tell her it was best if they kept their relationship professional.

The best defense was a good offense, that's what her dad had always told her and that's what she'd decided to do today.

Go on the offense. Get her revenge. Except she hadn't counted on the thrill of being back in the game and she couldn't stop her mind from whirling with so many ideas she'd stayed up into the early morning hours making notes.

She was back in the game, and not even Nathan's deception could temper her excitement.

****

"Geico has the gecko, Target has the bull's eye. Our job is to come up with a logo that will remind everyone of GS&I."

Nathan slipped into the boardroom and quietly took a chair in the corner. It'd been two long weeks since Dani had begun working for him. Two weeks of hell. But he'd played her game.

Sort of.

He couldn't keep from seeing her, so he'd come up with his own game plan that he smugly admitted was working to his advantage. No way was he allowing Ms. Danielle Hollis breathing room. He deliberately passed her in the hall, attended as many of her meetings as his schedule would allow, passed her office door as often as he could without looking like a fool. He kept her off guard and he could tell it was working.

Only he had noticed her slight hesitation when he'd walked into the room. As he sat back and crossed an ankle over a knee, he noted the color in her cheeks and the gleam in her eyes. It was obvious she loved what she was doing and he had to squash the spurt of anger when he thought of all William Delaney had taken from her.

"We need a brand," she was saying, although her words barely registered with him. It wasn't the words he was interested in. Dani Hollis knew what she was doing and he had all the faith in the world that she would take his company to the next level. "We want people to look at our logo and know it's us without having to tell them."

Today she wore red. A power color and she looked beautiful in it, although she still wore her hair in that tight twist and her makeup was perfect. He'd rather see the real Dani. The woman who'd exited the beat-up Datsun to face him in the middle of the street. But if Dani was anything, she was professional and he respected her need to dress in what she considered professional clothes. No way would he be like Delaney and tell her what to wear.

He glanced at his watch and rose, already late to his own meeting. As he stepped toward the door, their gazes collided, hers guarded, wary. He nodded and left, suppressing a smile of satisfaction and anticipation.

Hours later, Nathan was preparing to leave. The office had long since grown quiet, everyone having left to go home to families. He'd always hated this time of day because it made him feel like an outsider. There was no one to go home to, no one waiting for him. Since Dani had left him, his loneliness had grown more acute, nearly stifling. As he closed his office door and headed to the elevator, he noticed the wedge of light coming from her door.

More often than not, she stayed later than he and was in the office before him most mornings. For two weeks, he'd fought the urge to once again corner her in her office, demand she let him explain or at least speak to him. Tonight he stopped fighting and headed to her, even if it was just to say good night.

"Dani?" He pushed open the door. She was sitting at her desk, furiously making notes on a legal pad. Her head jerked up when he entered and her eyes grew round. Nathan propped his shoulder against the door jam. "You're here awfully late."

"Just making some notes. I'll be out of here soon." She tapped her pencil on the pad of paper.

"You okay?"

"Fine." The pencil continued tapping and he squashed the urge to take it from her.

"I miss you, Dani."

She sighed and dropped the pencil on the desk where it rolled to the edge of the paper. "Nathan..."

"I'm sorry for everything."

Their gazes locked. "Please, Nathan. Don't do this."

"Do what?" He pushed away from the doorframe and stepped up to her desk. She looked up at him, her eyes for once unguarded, filled with the pain of everything he had done to her. Seeing her suffering nearly brought him to his knees. "I'm so damn sorry, Dani."

Her lips thinned and he knew he was pushing his luck, treading where she didn't want him to go. "What's done is done," she said as she stood to face him.

"So that's it? I made a mistake and that's it? I can't be forgiven? I don't get a second chance?"

She hesitated and damn if his heart didn't turn over with hope. He pressed his advantage, grabbing the opportunity her hesitation provided. "I love you, Dani."

"Don't." She held up her hand as if she could stop his words. He merely took her hand in his and held on, the desk between them, but he

Accidental Love

didn't give a damn.

"Don't what? Don't admit my feelings? Don't tell you how I really feel? I didn't know what to do when I found out who you really were. I needed you, the company needed you, but there didn't seem to be a way to balance the two."

"Nathan..."

Using her trapped hand, he pulled her toward him. She came willingly, leaning across the desk until they were so close he could feel her breath on his face. "I love you," he whispered. "And I can't lose you."

He kissed her and nearly shouted in relief when she didn't pull away. When she kissed him back.

Slowly he released her, but she continued to lean across the desk, her eyes closed, her mouth moist with his kiss. Her eyes fluttered open until they were staring at each other. He wanted to kiss her again, but decided he'd done enough damage for one day.

He stepped back and Dani straightened, her expression confused and aroused.

"Don't work too late," he said, and turned away, fighting all the way to the elevator the voice inside him that said to turn back, to grab her and never let go.

****

As the elevator pinged its arrival, Dani slumped in her desk chair, her lips still tingling from Nathan's kiss. Damn him. Damn him, damn him, damn him.

She touched her lips with the tip of her finger and closed her eyes, not wanting to admit how much she'd wanted to crawl on top of the desk and pull him toward her. How much she'd missed him.

The past two weeks had been heaven and

hell. She loved what she was doing, eagerly awaited the hour until she could come back to work and see Nathan. No, no, no. Not see Nathan, to work on the campaign. She eagerly awaited *working on the campaign.*

With a sigh, she opened her eyes and dropped her hand to her lap. Who was she kidding? She loved her new job, but she really did rush into the office to see Nathan. She still loved him, damn it. After all he had done to her, she still loved him.

And what had he done?

He'd lied. He'd manipulated. He'd...

For some reason, she couldn't seem to conjure up her anger any more.

I didn't know what to do when I found out who you really were.

Could that be true? Was he as confused as she?

Yes, he had lied. Yes, he should have told her he'd been looking for her. He should have done a lot of things differently. Had he gotten in over his head? And when he found out why she was hiding, what could he have done? Expose her and bring William to her door?

Or hide her secret?

"Damn you, Nathan Gardner." He'd hidden her secret. He'd chosen her over his company.

She sighed and stared sightlessly at the opposite wall. She was such a fool, seeing only what she wanted to see, expecting the worse out of a man who had been nothing but kind and generous and loving.

The elevator pinged again and Dani jumped to her feet. Nathan had returned and she wasn't wasting another moment on her self-pity or her anger. She was going to tell him exactly how she felt.

Accidental Love

She was already out of her office and halfway down the hall by the time the elevator door swished open.

"Nathan, I lo..." She stumbled on her last words, her heart slamming against her ribs.

It wasn't Nathan who exited the elevator and headed toward her, but William.

For a moment, her mind went blank before it started racing at warp speed. Her instincts told her to run, but where? The offices were empty; Nathan had been the last to leave. A guard sat at the entrance fifteen floors down and she'd been here enough nights to know two others walked the floors, but Lord only knew where they were right now.

"Hello, Danielle." William stopped a few feet from her, his blonde head tilted as he stared at her. That voice she'd come to dread in her nightmares surrounded her and she found her tongue plastered to the roof of her mouth. Damn him for reducing her to a mass of Jell-o. "Red doesn't suit you," he said, his blue eyes taking a leisurely tour of her body, making her skin crawl.

She took a step back, but stopped herself from retreating farther. A show of defiance. She refused to give credence to those old feelings of inadequacy struggling to work their way up. "What are you doing here?" Her voice seemed unusually loud in the dark hallway.

"I heard a little rumor you were back in the business." His smile was cold. "I figured you wouldn't be able to stay away long."

William had always been one to wait patiently for his prey to come to him. She should have remembered that, but wondered if it really mattered. She was tired of hiding from him. Tired of being a coward.

"No rumor." She lifted her chin and his

white-blonde eyebrows rose mockingly.

"Your old employer has been wondering what happened to you. I had a hard time explaining that I had no idea where my fiancé had gone."

"I'm sure you came up with a plausible explanation."

The cold smile slipped and even in the dim light of the darkened hallway she could see the anger in his eyes, could feel it coming off him in waves. Her heart beat harder and she mentally catalogued the different escape routes.

"You embarrassed me, Danielle."

"Payback for all those times you embarrassed me." She infused her voice with as much sarcasm as she could while she tried not to remember each and every humiliation he'd heaped on her.

William's eyes narrowed. "You've changed, darling."

"For the better," she said, and almost laughed at the look of surprise he couldn't contain. Amazingly, it was that look that stiffened her back, reinforced her resolve. She wouldn't let William Delaney have a hold over her anymore. "I have a new job, a new life. Why don't you just go away?"

He took a step closer. The intimidation tactic worked, but she stood her ground, refusing to give him the satisfaction of seeing her back up. "I could ruin you, Danielle Hollis."

"Why, William? Why do you care about me? What do you want?"

He hesitated a moment, as if he had to wonder that himself. "You."

"Why would you want someone who clearly doesn't want to be with you?"

"Because you were mine. Because you

walked away. Because I didn't give you permission to leave."

She was amazed at his nerve, but even more appalled at the fact that he actually believed what he was saying. "You don't own me, William. I'm free to stay or go as I please."

He took another step closer until they were toe to toe. She took pride in the fact she didn't back up, didn't show fear. "But I do own you, Danielle. Without me to guide your career, you wouldn't be here now. You owe me."

She thought of all those nights he'd degraded her, all his insults over the months they'd been together, all the shame and embarrassment he'd caused. Everything came bubbling up, a suppressed anger she hadn't known existed, and she lashed out, striking William across the cheek, causing his head to whip to the side and a large, red welt to rise on his face.

Immediately she felt awful. She'd never hit anyone in her life and she was horrified that she'd let William drive her to this.

The anger in his eyes was like nothing she'd ever seen before. She pivoted on her high heels, but before she could make it a few feet, she was yanked backward by a hand in her hair. She cried out at the sharp pain in her scalp, stumbled, and fell against him. His arm snaked around her, pulled her in tight, one hand lodged in her hair, immobilizing her, the other against her throat, pressing against her windpipe until she began to wheeze and the hallway blurred.

Frantically, she clawed at his hands. He put his lips to her ear and whispered, "You made a mistake leaving me, Danielle."

She whimpered. Gone was her backbone, replaced with a frantic need to *breathe*, to run. Instead, she went limp. William grunted in surprise and his hands loosened enough that she could push away from him and start running down the hall. In the back of her mind, she dimly heard the elevator ping and she almost sobbed in relief. *Come on, come on,* she silently pled. *Open!* Behind her, she heard William yell out. She didn't have a chance unless those damn elevator doors opened. Slowly, they slid apart and Nathan leapt out.

"Dani!"

He grabbed her arm and shoved her behind him. Two guards exited the elevator, guns drawn, pointed at William who slid to a stop. His gaze darted between the guns and Dani who was leaning against the wall, alternately crying and breathing deep.

With an animalistic growl, Nathan lunged forward and tackled William. Both men went down in a pile of Armani and Hugo Boss, limbs tangled, punches thrown.

"Nathan!" Dani tried to pull him off as the guards pulled at William. Both men let go of each other. Nathan shrugged off her hand and straightened his jacket.

A guard took each of William's arms. He struggled against the hold, his perfectly combed hair falling in his eyes, the mark of her slap bright against his suddenly pale skin.

"Are you okay?" Nathan took her by the shoulders and looked her over.

Her smile was a bit wobbly, her throat hurt, and her scalp was numb where William had pulled her hair. "I'm fine."

"I saw him walk through the lobby on my way out, but it didn't register who he was until a few minutes later. I'm sorry I left you alone." He pulled her in for a swift hug, then released her, questions in his eyes.

Accidental Love

"I'm fine," she said again. Her body started to shake and the more she tried to stop it, the worse it got. Nathan threw his suit coat over her shoulders and immediately she was surrounded by his warmth and smell. The combination went a long way toward easing her fears.

It all happened quickly after that. The police arrived en masse, lights and sirens, as well as the media. This would be front-page news the next day and even though Nathan assured her it wasn't a problem, Dani felt horrible that GS&I had been dragged into her problems. Nathan urged her to go to the hospital, but she refused. Bruises were forming on her neck, but her injuries were superficial and she didn't want to go through the ordeal of the emergency room. Not when all she wanted was to crawl into bed.

William was hand cuffed and led away, sputtering and threatening to sue everyone in the building.

In the quiet aftermath, Dani and Nathan were left in the darkened building, facing each other.

"Are you sure you're okay?" Nathan asked, his eyes clouded with worry.

"I'm fine. I'm relieved it's over." She rubbed her arms, fighting a chill.

Nathan pulled her hands from her arms and held them in his. "Let's get you home."

****

"You still at the same apartment?" Nathan asked after they climbed into his Porsche.

Dani nodded, still unable to believe that William had attacked her. What could she have done differently? How could she have avoided it? Then she grew angry at herself. She was sick of blaming herself for everything William had done to her.

The drive to her apartment was silent, but oddly not uncomfortable. Dani stifled the urge to lean into Nathan's warmth and tried to block the images of William. When Nathan pulled up to the curb and cut the engine, they sat in silence. Dani looked up her apartment windows, not wanting to go in, wanting to stay with Nathan. But she refused to rely on another man again. She would fight her demons on her own for once. Reluctantly, she opened the door and stepped out. Nathan met her at the front of the newly restored Porsche. The streetlight above them hummed and cast a dim light over the cracked sidewalk.

"Come home with me," he said, his brows furrowed in worry. He touched her fingers. "Please, Dani. I'd feel better knowing you were near."

She shook her head. "I'll be okay."

His hand fell to his side and he turned. Together they walked to her door. "Call me if you need anything."

"I will." She tried to fit her key in the lock, but her hands were shaking too much and she missed.

"Damn it, Dani." Nathan took the keys from her and swiftly unlocked the door and swung it open. "It's okay to need someone," he said, his tone tinged with anger.

She hesitated before stepping inside, not able to look at him, embarrassed, once again, at what William had brought her to.

"Dani." He tilted her chin up until she looked at him. His lips tilted in a sad smile. "I'm glad you're okay, but did it ever occur to you that I'm not?"

She went still as his words sank in.

"You scared the hell out of me, sweetheart. I

don't think I'll ever truly get over seeing William chasing you down the hall. Maybe *I* need *you*, tonight."

Her tears ran over his thumb that was still holding her chin. "I'm sorry," she whispered.

"Ah, love." He pulled her into his embrace, held her tight while she fought her tears. "Don't ever be sorry for other's choices."

It was a lesson she was just beginning to learn, but with Nathan, she felt she could somehow overcome her past with William. Nathan led her into her apartment, switching the lights on as he went. He followed her to her bedroom and she realized this was the first time he'd ever stepped inside her home. Her clothes were strewn over her bed, a chair, the dresser, falling out of drawers and the closet. She didn't care.

Carefully, and with reverence, Nathan helped her change into her warmest, least sexy, pajamas, and tucked her into bed before shucking his own clothes down to his boxers and climbing in beside her to take her in his arms. He kissed her once on the top of the head, then tucked her head in the crook of his arm.

After some time she slept. And her dreams were peaceful.

When she awoke, the sun was streaming in through her window and Nathan was fast asleep beside her. She took her time observing him, watching. Loving. Slowly he came awake, his lashes fluttering, then rising. His eyes staring directly into hers. His smile was slow, but dazzling.

"Good morning," he said in his raspy, morning voice.

"Morning."

"Did you sleep well?"

"Very well," she admitted. "And you?"

He touched her hair, her cheek. "Very well."

They laid in silence, the sun's rays warming them until finally Dani asked the hard question. The one question that had been bothering her for weeks. "So what now?"

His gaze skimmed her face, so serious she had to suppress a shudder. "You tell me, Dani. What now?"

She licked her lips and looked away, not knowing how to voice her thoughts.

"I need to know that you're here, working for my company, because you want to be and not for revenge," he said.

Her gaze flew to his. "I'll be honest. It started out as revenge, but things have changed. I like what I'm doing. I like the people I work with." *I love you.*

He rolled to his side, went up on one elbow, and tucked a piece of her hair behind her ear, his gaze following the movement. "You're sure? This is what you want?"

She shrugged, though the movement was anything but offhand. "I want to get back into advertising." That much she knew for certain.

"You planning on leaving Cincinnati?"

Her head snapped up. "You planning on kicking me out?"

His eyes crinkled in a smile. "No. Just wondered where I would be following you."

Her throat went dry. "F-follow me?"

"Can't have my wife traipsing all over without me. I'd get lonely."

"Wife?"

"Wife. Lover. Whatever."

She narrowed her eyes. "What the hell is a whatever?"

Nathan threw back his head and laughed.

"Ah, Dani. I love you. So what do you say to a mutually agreeable settlement?"

She blinked. "Are you proposing marriage, Nathan Gardner, or renegotiating my contract? Which, by the way, has already been signed by your VP of Human Resources."

His lips twitched in another laugh. "Seeing as how I can't break that contract, I guess I'm suggesting marriage."

"Suggesting, huh?" She raised one eyebrow. "Suggesting?"

"Asking," he amended. "I'm asking. If you'd like to get married. Ah, hell." He growled and pulled her close in for a kiss that pummeled her already destroyed defenses and plundered her mouth. "Forget asking," he breathed into her ear. "I'm demanding. Be my wife, Danielle Hollis."

She laughed and brought him in for a quick kiss. "Well, if you put it that way. I have no choice but to accept."

If you enjoyed *Accidental Love*, you may also enjoy *Ellie's Delight* by Lea Winter
Following is the first chapter for your pleasure.

****

Chapter One

The last thing Gary said before Sterling Blalock left New York was, "Son, I think you need to have your head examined."

Looking back on the situation, Sterling started to think his assistant was right. As usual, Mr. Head Strong and Opinionated had to do things his own way, taking a vacation in the heartland.

"I want to get back to my roots." It sounded like a grand idea at the time. As Sterling glanced around, knee deep in the swatch of Middle America called Michigan, he wondered if the idea was so grand after all.

"Might as well make the best of it," he muttered under his breath, as he hailed a cab and jumped in.

Hovering on the edge of the seat, his knee bounced with nervous anticipation and he addressed the stout cabby with his usual no nonsense attitude. "Hey, Mack. How far is this place I'm headed to, anyway?"

"The name's Ed, and it's only another five or ten minutes. It's not too far outside of Flint. You coming home to see family?" The cabby slouched comfortably, his heavy frame blending into the faded upholstery of the cab's leather interior. It was a wonder he could see the road.

"Nope. It's a vacation. I needed some down time." Sterling craned his neck to watch a flock of sheep and wondered what type of exotic stew would taste good with the addition of lamb.

Sneak Preview Ellie's Delight by Lea Winter

Funny, he had the impression Flint, Michigan was more of an industrial center. He never imagined it would be flanked by farmland.

"If I ever get a vacation, it's gonna be to some place nice, like Hawaii. Not some half-frozen wasteland like here," the cabby commented, playing with the dials on his two-way radio.

Sterling thought back on the warmth of Hawaii as he watched white patches, half-snow, half-ice, dot the road. Maybe Hawaii would have been a better choice. He didn't remember the Midwest being this cold. The cabby was right. He could be lying on a beach with his arms and lips wrapped around some luscious island babe. The thought was becoming more appealing by the minute. "Thanks, I'll keep it in mind for the next time."

"Alright, Pal. We're almost to your stop. That'll be $32.50. I'm gonna give you my card in case you decide to hightail it back to wherever it is you call home. Just ring. I'll come get you."

As the house came into view, Sterling lurched forward, his arms draped over the front seat. Somehow, he hadn't pictured the bi-level banana yellow structure standing before him. It was an old dwelling, built on a wooden frame, but it was well maintained and looked as if it had just been given a fresh coat of paint.

Sterling slid the wallet out of his back pocket and handed the driver two twenties. "Keep the change." He grabbed his duffle bag and let himself out.

The driver nodded as he shoved a business card out the window. "Remember, I'll come get you if you want me to." The cabby gestured a quick salute and sped out of sight.

Sterling took a deep breath as he slid the

card into the inside pocket of his jacket and his heart sank as he spied an old Ford truck. He couldn't remember the last time he rode in a vehicle so dilapidated.

Dark blue paint flaked off in pancake-sized spots. Someone had tried to arrest the rust with sanding and poorly applied globs of Bondo. One thing was certain—any delusion of the comforts of New York had been brushed away.

He started up the slender cement path. It was now or never. His pace slowed as he took the stairs in a relaxed manner. Ignoring the doorbell, Sterling raised his hand to knock on the heavy wooden frame.

His hostess was probably some sweet but plain girl he would learn to feel comfortable with in a few days. He laughed to himself and rapped lightly.

"One moment, please. I'm just pulling a pie out of the oven."

The voice was soft and laced with seduction, like the song of a siren to a sailor far from home.

Again, thoughts of the woman behind the door filled his mind. He pictured a frail young miss, her greatest asset her voice, dressed in a red and white gingham skirt, covered from her neck to her knees in an apron. Some sweet little thing with freckles and pigtails...and a face only her mother could love.

He placed the heavy bag on the porch, shifted his weight to a ready stance as he glanced around, and wondered if he had enough time to turn and run. When he was at the airport, he saw a return flight to New York scheduled for later that night. If he left now, he could leave an envelope with the rental money in her mailbox and the whole thing would be over.

In his moments of waiting, he wondered if he needed a vacation as badly as he thought. What

Sneak Preview Ellie's Delight by Lea Winter

was taking her so long? Was her oven located in the next county? It was rare a woman made him wait for anything, and here he was playing second fiddle to a pie.

As the door swung open, he almost dropped the straps of his duffel bag to the porch. Standing before him was a vision dressed in blue. A dark haired angel with soft shoulder length curls and big, welcoming doe eyes that smiled. She had full pouting lips, the type he could see himself kissing for hours, and high cheekbones so delicate they made his heart skip a beat.

His eyes lingered on the pleasant lines of her face, traveling down the soft folds of blue material, drinking in the way it clung to her full breasts. The dress tapered to a slight waist, giving way to rounded hips. He liked a woman with a real figure. He was tired of rail-thin beauties and New York was full of them.

Why was he responding to her this way? He had dozens of women at his disposal day and night and not one of them had this effect on him. He pulled the duffel bag in front of his body and extended a hand in greeting.

"Ste...ste..." Sterling stammered. In his excitement, he almost introduced himself in his most familiar manner.

"Stuart Black?" Ellie asked, awkwardly.

"Yeah. I guess I was somewhere else for a second. I'm your housemate for the next month." Stuart smiled as his eyes lingered on the woman in front of him. One slip-of-the-tongue would be one too many. It would cost him his long awaited vacation. He had to be conscious of where he was and who he was supposed to be, but that wouldn't be easy with his hostess around. God, she was beautiful.

"Pleased to meet you. Eleanor Burton, but

all my friends call me Ellie." She offered her hand with a delicate grip, motioning left for her guest to enter.

Stuart touched Ellie's arm with a friendly gesture and the pulse in his groin quickened. The softness of her skin, paired with the delicate scent of baby powder, affected him in ways he never dreamed possible. He checked this emotion deftly and stepped past her, entering the house.

He was no stranger to passionate feelings, but usually they weren't attached to something as innocent as a first meeting. He didn't believe in love at first sight. It had been a long day and he was certain the stress of the trip had gotten to him.

****

If she had known he was so attractive, she might have said "no" to Gary's request. She suppressed the urge to giggle—at least she was able to hide her surprise a little better than her guest, but she was no less inspired. She felt nervous as a schoolgirl watching the strong line of the star quarterback's jaw, but it wasn't his jaw she was admiring. Her eyes rose slowly to meet his, unified in awkwardness, broken only by his timely, obligatory smile.

The man in her doorway towered over her, his slender physique athletically muscular. Though he was dressed in jeans, a leather jacket, and an "I love New York" T-shirt laboring to accommodate the muscles of his chest, he carried himself with extreme composure, and self-confidence. She guessed him to be ten years older than the eighteen or nineteen year old she had imagined, but that wasn't necessarily a bad thing.

Pale gray eyes the color of a polished dime held her mesmerized as they peered at her from under tussled tufts of blue-black waves, curling around his ears. For a moment, she worried she had spilled cooked rhubarb on the front of her dress. As she gazed down to check, her eyes were drawn again to the tightness of his jeans and the way they held evidence of his approval for her in check.

This time, her cheeks flushed with color as she wondered if he responded to every woman he met in the same way. Funny, Alan was the last man to look at her with such obvious lust. It would take time for her to get used to the idea of having a young, attractive man living under her roof.

The newcomer entered the house swiftly, his cultivated swagger brimming with confidence. He dropped the bag next to the coffee table, pulled his jacket off, and after taking a seat on the couch, laid the coat across his all-too-obvious erection.

"Thanks for letting me crash here for a while," he said, while looking around at his surroundings.

Light flooded the room through a bay window, as the cream and brown decor sparkled with warmth. The room was immaculate, and though it was sparsely decorated, the pieces were well chosen for the space they occupied.

Stuart sniffed the air, his worried expression replaced by a faint curl of a smile. "Strawberry-rhubarb pie..." His words were mumbled and meant to be more of a thought than something voiced aloud.

"Yes. I thought it might be a nice way to welcome you to Lake Sycamore." Ellie's face was radiant as she reached toward him, offering to take the jacket.

He lifted the leather from his settling embarrassment and rummaged through the pockets until he removed a pack of Marlboros and a lighter. Pounding the pack roughly against his left hand, he stopped upon seeing the look on her face.

"What?"

"I hope you don't plan on smoking in here." She was dead serious.

"That was the plan, but I see things have changed."

"You're more than welcome to step out on the front porch," Ellie replied, trying to sound pleasant.

"As if I have a choice," he quipped, returning the unlit stick to the cigarette box. "Maybe later."

****

So much for great first impressions, he thought as he extended his arm to offer her the coat. He watched as Ellie walked to the wooden rack by the door. The mischievous grin returned to his face, amused by the movement of her hips as they jostled the delicate fabric of the blue dress. The view was almost worth giving up the cigarette.

She walked toward the back of the living room, ascending the bottom step of a carpeted staircase. "Come on. I'll show you where you'll stay."

Feeling more settled, Stuart hiked the duffel bag across his shoulder and followed his hostess. His eyes played the rhythm of her body instead of paying attention to the stairs and he stumbled, barely saving himself by grabbing the railing as a stifled curse made her turn to face him.

Her brow wrinkled with concern more than disdain, though she didn't say a word. Her lips parted as if she was going to speak, but after sizing up the situation she continued up the stairs.

Stuart rolled his eyes. Stumbling was more

embarrassing than the erection had been. He issued himself a silent word of caution. He was in the country for rest and relaxation, not for a forbidden affair with some country beauty.

In New York, he avoided things that distracted him from his work, and as far as he could tell, Ellie Burton had a way of distracting him from everything.

****

She didn't need to give him a tour of the upstairs—the area was so small every room was self-evident. He urged her to return to whatever she was doing before his arrival and she nodded, disappearing down the stairs.

He peered at the antiquated bathroom with its iron fixtures and make-shift shower and wished he was at home staring at a marble and gold setup boasting five showerheads.

"It could be worse," he scolded under his breath as he turned on the running water in the sink initiating a myriad of bumping and popping sounds. "I can't believe I was pining for the country and dying to get back to my roots. I've got a mind to..." Stuart turned the fixture hard to stop the flow of water as a lavender room, delicate with feminine mystique caught his eye.

It had to be Ellie's room. He knew he shouldn't snoop—his hostess was entitled to her privacy. Still, one quick peek couldn't hurt.

A four-poster bed draped in a white and purple quilt sat atop an alabaster carpet. The starkness of the rug stopped him where he stood and prompted him to take two steps back for fear of disturbing its gentle solitude. He leaned into the door to get a better look.

In the far right corner of the room sat an old-fashioned white vanity with a matching upright mirror. Lace valances draped the windows and a snow-white bureau was topped with a variety of teddy bears keeping silent guard on an intricate lace doily. The bears only added to the virginal pattern of the pristine room, a continuance of white-on-white surrounded by soft purple hues.

Content with a quick glimpse into a special part of his hostess' life, he returned to his room and started to unpack the duffel bag.

"Everyone makes such a big deal about smoking. Can't smoke in my office, thought it might be different here, but no. Jeez." Stuart tossed his T-shirts onto the double bed.

He tried to think back on what had prompted him to return to the country and for the life of him, he couldn't remember. He was happy in New York. He had everything a man could want. Still, it seemed something was missing from his life. Sometimes he thought about what it would be like to take a wife, to have four little rug rats playing at his feet.

"Fat chance," he snorted, with a quick chuckle. No matter how much he thought about it, he knew in his heart he wasn't that type of guy. Black Beane Foods was his family. He lived for the time it took to nurture her and make her the most powerful entity she could be. He knew in that respect he was exactly like his uncle.

He stopped for a second to admire the solid craftsmanship of an ornate iron footlocker at the end of the bed. The little boy inside of him expected the old chest to house some unexpected treasure. He propped the lid up, careful not to make any loud noises in the process. He wasn't sure how his hostess would take his going through the chest, but since she hadn't directed him not to, he was sure it was available for inspection.

He peered deep into the trunk and the strong odor of cedar chips attacked his nostrils. It looked empty; all except for something bundled in a blanket. Stuart leaned into the chest, careful to make a mental note on the exact way the parcel was packaged.

What's the fun in being nosy if you get caught doing it? He would be certain to put everything back exactly the way it had come out, after he inspected it thoroughly.

He pulled the package into his lap and settled back into the feather softness of the bed. The red plaid brought a smile to his lip—his aunt had a blanket made of the same pattern when he was small. The bundle was wrapped with such care and precision, he was certain he had stumbled upon some prized possession.

He glanced toward the door. The last thing he wanted was to get caught snooping, like some old lady. It just wasn't becoming of a corporate CEO. Then again, he could think of worse things his curiosity had gotten him into.

He unfolded the blanket to find a white dress shirt atop a black suit jacket with matching pants cradling a pair of men's black dress shoes. As he stared at the clothing, a framed photo slipped out from the folds and, if it weren't for his quick reflexes, it would have hit the floor shattering into a million pieces. He looked toward the door, teeth clenched and his face distorted with guilt, as the heavy object rested in his hands.

The photo seemed to stare back at him, pulling him into its space and sparking emotions foreign to his being. Ellie was at its center with both arms draped around the neck of an amiable-looking red-haired bloke who grinned from ear-to-ear. Stuart stared deeper into the frame. It was Ellie, all right. And she looked happy—more than happy—she was elated.

He didn't know why, but seeing Ellie with some good-looking stud made a knot the size of Cleveland form in the pit of his stomach. He tucked the photo back under the suit and began to wrap the treasured bundle the way it had been before he removed it from its resting place.

"Come on," he chastised. "Why should I be jealous of Ellie and her male friend? It's just a photo and I don't even know the woman. Everyone has a life and people in it who make it worth living." He placed everything as it had been and closed the lid on the chest. "I could have that type of life, but I choose not to. Besides, I'm too busy to get involved with anyone. I'm smart enough to know I can do without the hassle."

He could tell himself a million times he was happy, but deep inside, there was no denying something was missing. Stuart started to think he would have been better off leaving the chest alone. He hated when loneliness made him feel self-effacing.

He realized a long time ago, sharing life with someone didn't make it better or anymore worthwhile. As far as he could tell, it meant aggravation and pretenses that shattered like a dropped ornament when challenged, leaving both parties feeling worse than before the whole mess started. As for Ellie, if this man still meant as much to her as he once did, Stuart was certain he would be meeting Mr. Perfect sooner or later.

He pushed the chest from his mind, enjoying the bounce of the feather softness of the bed. As he looked around, he realized the starkness of the room was oddly disturbing. Even as a youth in Indiana he had more furniture in his bedroom than was in the rented room. It was as if it had been stripped down to bare necessities.

"Seems she needs a renter more than I need

Sneak Preview Ellie's Delight by Lea Winter

a vacation," he spouted with amusement. He chose to shrug it off—it was none of his business. He was staying for a relatively short time. He would simply make do. He would use the mirror in the bathroom for grooming and, if there were something more he needed, he had a credit card and his checkbook tucked inside his duffle.

His immediate concern was finding out just how lonely the beautiful woman downstairs was. He didn't need fancy furniture to show her a good time. And he was aching to see if he could break his record time for seduction of four hours.

Thank you for purchasing this Wild Rose Press publication. For other wonderful stories of romance, please visit our on-line bookstore at
www.thewildrosepress.com.

For questions or more information contact us at
info@thewildrosepress.com.

The Wild Rose Press
www.TheWildRosePress.com